A View from the Roof

stories by

Helen Weinzweig

Goose Lane Editions

Published with the assistance of the Canada Council, and the
University of New Brunswick, 1989.

Cover illustration, "Face" by Stephen May
Book design by Julie Scriver
Printed in Canada by Wilson Printing

Canadian Cataloguing in Publication Data

Weinzweig, Helen 1915-
A view from the roof

ISBN 0-86492-110-1

I. Title.

PS8595.E36V53 1989   C813'.54   C89-09654-1
PR9199.3.W44V53 1989

Goose Lane Editions Ltd.
248 Brunswick Street,
Fredericton, New Brunswick
Canada E3B 1G9

CONTENTS

PREFACE

Artistic development is at least as organic as it is sequential, and in the realm of short fiction, a thematic arrangement of an author's work can be as illuminating as a more conventional ordering in sequence of publication. While the *Collected Stories* of such able practitioners as Elizabeth Bowen and John Cheever are presented in the strictest chronology, as equally lauded a writer as Graham Greene ends his complete "escapades" with "End of the Party," one of his earliest—and best—ventures.

The thirteen works which comprise this near-complete collection of Helen Weinzweig's stories invite the sharper focus provided by an imaginative structure. Her ruefully witty and mordant treatment of various Jewish-Gentile collisions, both comic and serious, threads throughout the opening cluster of eight stories. The last two of these, "L'Envoi" and "A View from the Roof," fuse Semitic concerns with Weinzweig's ubiquitous interest in the life of the artist—a preoccupation later and perhaps most suggestively documented in "Journey to Porquis."

Weinzweig's role as one of Canada's most contemporary writers manifests itself clearly in the experimentation of the last five stories, which also maintain and deepen her incisive analyses of psychic and marital unease. The collection closes with one of her strongest offerings, "The Man Without Memories," a tale about a man trying to reduce the flux of life to an art-like ritual—not unlike Sophie from the opening story, "Circle of Fifths," who cleaves to the "furious" polonaise of Chopin and the comforts of a Bach concerto.

In his Introduction to *English Letters of the XVIII Century* James Aitken writes, "with a small mirror one may catch a glimpse of a wide scene." Continued re-readings of *A View from the Roof* will reveal how very wide the scene this small mirror holds.

John Timmins

CIRCLE OF FIFTHS

There was a time in the 1960s when a million tourists came to New York City every day. They came to see the Babylon of the New World. Flashed on movie screens everywhere were the names of four mythical cities signifying international fame: New York, London, Paris, Rome. Well, in 1938 I had no money to seek international fame in Europe, so I went to New York to study music. Later, with a small (in international terms) career going and a loving husband, I stayed on to become a "native" New Yorker.

As an expatriate Canadian, I was sometimes called upon to offer shelter to visitors. We didn't mind providing the welcome, a guest room in our Washington Heights apartment, clean towels, and a map. The city took over and did the rest. I enjoyed this way of seeing old friends and relations, since little was asked of me except to share their excitement of discovery.

From Toronto came my old friend Rita Simpson, née Krushelniki. We had grown up in Weyburn and had considered one another best friends. I had not seen or heard from Rita since the Depression dispersed us like seeds before the hot winds of a prairie drought. Our own parched land could not hold us, and we drifted to take root elsewhere: I to New York, Rita to Toronto. Despite the vast distances between cities, immigrant families have a way of keeping track of their own. Therefore I knew that Rita had married well—an expression used by my aunts to let me know that, unlike me, my former friend was rich.

Rita phoned one night from the Plaza. Why, I demanded, hadn't she let me know she was coming?

"I wasn't sure I wanted to see you."

Well, I thought, so they still practise honesty back home.

"What made you change your mind?" I was slightly miffed.

"I didn't want to see anyone I know. But I have to. I'm so lost. I thought if I was alone, yet with lots of people around, I would find out—I might discover—honestly, I don't know what I thought would happen. I feel awful, so damned alone. Maybe with you I can pretend to be who I used to be or who I think I used to be. Oh God, I don't know anything anymore."

I resisted the temptation to ask what else is new. After twenty-five years in New York I was up to the top of my greying head in characters searching for lost identities. I made no comment, because I remembered that in Canada we were reputed to be slightly backward, lagging behind the States in everything. Where I come from they are probably just entering the Age of Anxiety.

*

The next day after work I stood in the lobby of the Plaza, trying to find a woman of about forty-five who would fit my memory of Rita. "Sooo-oo—phiee. . . !" came a call, loud and clear. Obviously, Rita did not intend to remain unnoticed while alienated. She waited just long enough for every head to turn and locate the source of the disturbance. Then, as everyone watched, she ran, not too quickly, across the lobby. She hugged me and sniffed back the tears.

"Darling! Dear, darling Sophie, how wonderful to see you, you haven't changed a bit, not at all. I'm so glad someone in this crazy world has stayed the same."

I sighed. Staying the same meant, I supposed, that I was not in fashion. I still pulled my straight hair back into a bun; I used no make-up; and stood firmly in flat-heeled Oxfords.

"All set, checked out?" I asked. "Then let's go."

"Sweetie, couldn't we stay uptown and have dinner? We could go to some fancy restaurant, have a good talk, just you and I, do you realize it's been almost twenty-five years since we talked, really *talked*."

"We can't do that," I told her. "Phil is waiting."

"It's almost seven. Wouldn't it be better to phone him not to wait for you?"

"No, no we eat late. Phil has to have a hot bath and a change of clothes when he gets home. Then he reads a while to relax. When he's ready, we eat."

"Poor man," said Rita. "he must have to work very hard. What does he do, construction, machine shop, something like that?"

I smiled at the thought of my husband permitting dirt to get under his fingernails.

"He's a lawyer," I told her, "in the city's tax department."

In the cab I tried to cheer her up; she seemed a bit let down.

"You will like Phil, everyone loves him. He's sensitive and kind. And I know you will appreciate his fine mind. He's brilliant, and so patient with me. You remember what a dope I was at school. All I could do was play the piano."

"All you could do!" she repeated. "Why you would have been a great concert pianist if it hadn't been for the Depression."

True or not, I loved her for thinking so. It had been a long time since anyone, myself included, had indicated such faith in my former talents.

On our way up to the apartment, I warned Rita never to ride alone in the elevator.

"Telephone ahead and Phil or I will meet you downstairs and come up with you. Sometimes women are molested in the elevators."

She giggled and said she wouldn't mind, it would be a change.

While I was unlocking our door, she remarked—as I knew she would, since we both were raised in a small western community where dependence led to trust—"That's four keys you used. Good lord, what do you keep in this apartment? The Russian crown jewels?" Then, as we stood in the dark and I waved my hand in the air for the string attached to the light fixture, she added, "When did you convert from coal-oil?"

I ignored the sarcasm. People who do not live in New York have no idea what we're up against.

"Honey," I told her, "you might as well learn the facts of big city life right now. I'm sorry we can't give you a set of keys while you're here. Three of the keys can be duplicated, but the fourth is for a special burglar-proof bar that goes across the door inside. It's installed by the police department. They keep one key and Phil or I have the other. It's not as inconvenient as it sounds, since Phil and I go everywhere together. What we'll do, you and I, is co-ordinate our plans. No problem."

We carried our luggage in. I called out to Phil. When I introduced them, my husband and my friend took each other's measure over a lingering handshake. Then Phil bent down to pick up the suitcases and noticed Rita's stiletto heels digging into the broadloom.

"You can't wear shoes like that in here," he said.

Rita stared thoughtfully at Phil as she considered one retort after another, the nature of her unexpressed replies being quite clear in the way her mouth twisted. She swallowed her scorn. With two high vigorous kicks she sent the offending pumps flying down the end of the long hall. Quickly I handed her a pair of straw slippers we keep for wet weather.

When, a little later, we sat down to dinner, Phil and Rita looked over each other's heads. Silently, we began to eat.

"Almost forgot," Rita jumped up, "brought you something." And came back with a bottle of Scotch.

"The best you can get," she said, unscrewing the bottle. "Cheers, my dears. Leave us have a cheery toast on this too, too solemn occasion."

She handed the bottle to Phil, he looked toward me.

"Please don't misunderstand," I said, "we appreciate the gift, but we can't accept it. We never indulge."

"And I bet you don't drink either." She laughed. We didn't. "It wouldn't hurt lover-boy here to take a drink, might thaw the icicles." She shrugged. "But do what you like with the stuff; I'm not taking it back."

Without hesitation, Phil grasped the open bottle firmly by the neck and turned it upside down over the sink. Twenty-six ounces of Bell's Royal Reserve gurgled a choked protest into the sewers. You could barely breathe. Alcohol fumes mixed with the garlic in the stew; Rita's strong perfume lost out in the competition. My little kitchen, which someone once called clinical, smelt like a cheap bar. Phil got one of his coughing spells and had to go and lie down. Rita looked as empty as the bottle.

"Come on, sweetie," I said, "I'll play for you. You always liked Chopin, remember?"

In my studio, Rita recognized some things I had brought from home after my mother died. She stroked the mahogany of the first grand piano in Weyburn; she held to her face the old, red silk Spanish shawl that had been the only colour in our drab parlour. I took my time, pretending to search for music I knew as well as my mother's name.

"Oh, now I remember!" Rita became euphoric. A Slav uses memory as a tranquilizer, to by-pass anguish, to blur reality. "Most of all I remember your mother. They don't build them like your mother any more. I used to sink into that big fat chest of hers like into a feather bed. 'Never mind, kitten,' she used to say, 'this trouble will pass.' Then she'd give me a big hug and something to eat. Whether I was hungry or not, I had to eat. Then you would play for me. To this day, I cry when I hear your recital pieces. I don't suppose we ever lose the emotions we had in our youth; we just cover them up as if we were cats who had soiled in the sand."

"My mother was an angel," I recalled. "She took in every stray cat on the street."

Rita's distant smile vanished. She spoke slowly.

"Is that what your mother thought I was—just a stray alley cat? All the time I thought it was *me*, particularly me, Rita, she loved."

What could I say to this middle-aged, motherless child. I am no one's mother, I thought, and I will not be yours. I played Chopin, instead. Furiously, *The Polonaise*, then some preludes. I played for Rita, for my dead parents; I played for loneliness, for everyone's aloneness. Then Phil came into the room, and while my husband and my friend stood side by side at the piano, listening to what my music had to tell them, I changed to valses and nocturnes, playing quietly now, and all from memory.

*

Fortunately, I have always had my music to turn to. I do not feel so barren once I get into a Bach concerto. I feel sorry for many of my generation, the Depression types, who

have nothing to take hold of. They seem always to be dissatisfied, forever hoping to get a life's worth, as it were,
from someone else's experiences. They are the kind of
people who trip over bricks while talking about the con-
cepts of modern architecture. They have remained
perennial school children with hands raised.

While we ate dinner, Phil and Rita wandered happily
through the schoolyard of their minds. Each had taken in-
numerable courses; each had read too much. I sat and
listened to a lot of palaver about Zen and Existentialism,
French poetry and Pop Art. Phil was excited to have such
a receptive audience; and Rita, I could tell, played up to
him, flattering him with an intense stare into his eyes. At
midnight I called a halt.

"Look, you two," I said, "some of us have to go to work
in the morning."

I took Rita to the guest room. She sat on the edge of
the bed and patted a spot beside her.

"Stay a minute and talk to me," she said.

"I can't honey, it's too late. Tomorrow is a very long day
for me. I teach five classes in Long Island."

She didn't hear me.

"Sophie, what am I like now?" she asked. "I mean, how
do I appear to you, have I changed much as a person, I
mean, not physically."

I recognized the familiar soul-searching gambit, and although I'm not an unsympathetic person, I really was too
tired for the old game of who-am-I-what-am-I.

"We'll have a chat tomorrow night," I promised.

"I'm going out tomorrow night, to the theatre. Sophie,
just a few minutes, please? . . . Don't you remember how we
used to stay awake talking most of the night?"

"That was in our careless youth. Phil has to have his
rest, too."

Helen Weinzweig

"So let him."

"You don't understand. He can't go to sleep unless I'm beside him."

She shrugged acceptance. Then, "Goddamn together-ness," she muttered, and without another look in my direction, went into the bathroom. My "goodnight, dear," was lost in the rush of water into the tub.

*

The next night Rita went to a Broadway play, and Phil and I went to bed early. He promptly fell asleep, and I de-cided to read while waiting up for Rita. I kept checking the little clock against the estimated time the theatre would be out. At one o'clock she still had not phoned. I held the book, I turned the pages; but not a word I read got past the images of Rita. How *had* she appeared to me? To tell the truth, she reminded me of some of those wealthy matrons whose children I taught. The youthful matriarchs sat about in the living room and drank cocktails, while I was downstairs in the rumpus room, coping with their indifferent offspring. To me, these women seemed to be selfish creatures who did precious little to earn their bed, board, and station wag-ons. Rita had the same air of self-centredness, a way of always holding onto an inner, apprehensive core. She ap-peared to be without ties of any kind: she had not mentioned her husband or her three children.

Phil woke up and said for pete's sake turn out that light.

"Rita hasn't come back," I told him.

"Who? She what?"

"I said, Rita hasn't come home from the theatre."

"What time is it?"

"After two. I'm worried."

"Didn't she phone?"

"That's just it, I haven't heard from her at all. I'm really worried."

"When did you see her last, what did she say?"

"This morning. We took the subway together. I wrote out directions for the galleries—you know, the Guggenheim, the Metropolitan, the Museum of Modern Art—then she was going to stay uptown and have her dinner and go on to the theatre. I made her promise not to try the subway on her own, to take a cab. She was terribly intrigued with the subway, maybe she took it anyway, she could be in Brooklyn by now."

"Wherever she is, she could have phoned."

"What if something has happened to her?"

"We would have heard."

"I'm not so sure. The way people avoid getting involved these days, you could die a slow death in front of a hundred onlookers and all they would do is stand and watch while rigor mortis set in."

"The police would have called us if she were hurt."

"Suppose she was mugged and her purse stolen. Our number isn't listed and she would have no way of getting in touch with us. Really, I'll never understand why you insist on an unlisted phone. We're not that rich or that famous that we should be disturbed by unwanted calls."

"We're not going to discuss that again. I will not have my telephone number printed and handy for some lunatic to have sport with. Anyway, nothing we can do about Rita right now. If we begin to check all the hospitals and police stations, we'd tie up the line for the rest of the night. We have to keep the line open just in case she does call. She will either be back, or we'll hear from her. If not, we'll look into the matter systematically first thing in the morning."

For the rest of the night we kept urging one another to go to sleep, but all we did was mutter about not being able to sleep. We listened to the sirens howling up Amsterdam Avenue. We followed the high hysterical pitch, relieved when the sound went past our corner. It is sad, but this city teaches you not to send to know for whom the siren screams, so long as it does not scream for thee or me. At dawn, normal noise began to break the fearful silence— New York's own anvil chorus of automobile horns in the street.

"People come to New York," I said, "and do not realize how different this city is from their home town. When I went into the Plaza yesterday to get Rita, there she was, in the middle of a dozen people, all strangers I'm sure, chattering away as if she were at the YWCA in Weyburn. I remember when we were about eighteen we went job-hunting together. On the streetcar she sat beside a young man and started to read his newspaper. I was standing in front of them, hanging on to the strap, and could see they were both looking at the want ads, like an old married couple. She always had a tendency towards instant intimacy. She asked him, just like that, 'Can you type?' He said, 'A little,' and she said, 'Why not come with us, maybe they'll hire a man if they can get him for the same salary as a girl.' He came along and was the only male in the line-up and, sure enough, landed the job. She thought she had been very clever. 'We never had a chance anyway,' she said, 'maybe now he can afford to marry some nice girl. Just think, Sophie, I may be responsible for a big happy family!' It never occurred to me yesterday to warn her against speaking to strangers. That's something you tell a child."

*

It was eight a.m. before the downstairs bell rang—a sound my straining ears welcomed as if it were Handel's "Hallelujah Chorus."

"Greetings, my darlings," Rita said lightly, "glad I got back before you left for work. I'm dead."

I winced at that word. It was a blessed fact that Rita was alive, yet she was more ectoplasm than solid flesh. Her skin was grey, her unseeing eyes were lost in dark sockets. From her spirit world we heard,

"Must get some sleep. See you later."

"Look here," Phil started after her, "what happened to you? Where were you?"

The zombie moved rigidly toward her room.

"I'm leaving my door open so's I can hear the phone." Her mask softened into a coy, silly smile. "I'm expecting a very important call. Cheers, dears."

Phil said, "I don't understand. Where does she think she is—at the Plaza? And you, you Sophie, you just stand there, without a word. She's supposed to be a friend of yours, yet she hasn't shown you the slightest consideration. Where did she spend the night? Not a word. No apology, nothing. Sure, you were buddy-buddies in some godforsaken wilderness a hundred years ago, but that doesn't give her the right to treat you without respect. I will not tolerate such behaviour in my home. She'll have to leave. Right now." And headed for the guest room.

"You Americans," I said distinctly. That stopped him. "You Americans think you own everything and everyone. You do the same thing all over the world: offer with one hand and steal with the other."

"There you go again, confusing a cultural complex with individual normative behaviour. I give up. I'm going back to bed."

"You still have time to get to work."

"Your *non sequiturs* slay me."

"What's that got to do with being late for work?"

"Exactly. Call the office and tell them I'm sick."

He was closer to the truth than he knew. Big, red blotches had appeared behind his ears and on the back of his neck. In a couple of hours his whole body would be covered with a rash. He would have a slight temperature and be sick to his stomach. Phil's cousin, the doctor, told me that these symptoms could be described as the only-child-about-to-have-a-tantrum syndrome.

When we three met again, it was late afternoon. We wandered into the kitchen in pyjamas and housecoats. Rita wore some trailing stuff we kept stepping on. We moved sluggishly around one another, taking turns at the window to stare out at the rain. The heavy downpour was ineffectual against the thick black smoke from a thousand chimneys below. Phil looked very stern. A few times he attempted an agitated stride but was defeated by the small space.

Phil thinks because he went to a few lectures he knows all about role-playing. Actually, my people invented the technique in the Ukraine. Rita was giving dimension to an act familiar to me: she was all three of Chekhov's sisters. Her sights were on some Moscow. She brooded and yearned; she cried a little and laughed a little; she was desperate; she was resigned; she suffered—oh how she could suffer. My method is to make music or serve food.

"We'll have a good, nourishing lunch," I announced.

"All I want's coffee," Rita murmured.

"We never drink coffee."

"For heaven's sake, Sophie, what's happened to you? We were weaned on the wine in your father's cellar." Rita threw up her hands. "I guess I'd better dress and go out for a cup of strong, black coffee." She rose, then sat down again. "No, I can't; I'm afraid to miss that call."

"Do you mean that you are actually having your lover telephone you here, to my house?" Phil demanded.

"He's not my lover," Rita said.

"Aha, then there is a man!" My husband, the lawyer, was triumphant.

"Eat," I ordered.

"This dried cow-dung is delicious," Rita muttered.

"Stop that kind of talk," I reprimanded her.

"Make him stop his kind of talk," Rita kept her eyes on her plate.

"Then you admit you were out all night with a man." Phil persisted, as if he were standing proxy for Rita's husband.

"Not in that tone of voice I wasn't."

"Who is he?"

"I don't know."

"Do you mean to tell me that you actually spent the night with a man whose name you don't even know?"

"I don't know his name, yet I know who he is. I mean, I don't know him, but I know *him*."

"You're not making sense."

"That's the way it is. That's the way it's always been. I see what others won't recognize."

"That's a dangerous rationalization. The mental wards are full of nuts with private visions. But that's your problem. I just want to make sure you're not going to drag me and my wife into a scandal."

"You must believe me—I have done nothing to be ashamed of."

"You're lying!"

At first I thought Phil was merely flexing a few professional muscles. After all, he never gets a chance to exercise before a witness. I expected Rita to counter his cross-examination with some flippant evasion; instead, she was backing away from her inquisitor, pressed small against the chair. I broke in:

"You know, Rita, you had us very upset. Phil is just as concerned about you as I am. You didn't come home last night, you never telephoned, what were we to think? You still haven't told us just what did happen to you."

"I know, and I'm sorry. By the time it occurred to me to get in touch with you, it was very, very late. I didn't want to wake you, and I had no key, so we figured it was the point of no return and decided to stay up the rest of the night. What's more, we were miles from a telephone."

"Where was that?" Phil demanded.

"Oh, somewhere in the middle of Central Park."

Phil seemed caught between outrage and disbelief. I tried appeasement. "But she is back, safe here with us."

Rita continued, "Isn't it a beautiful park? Why, you would never expect to find this lovely sanctuary in the heart of such a vast desert of concrete. There was no one about. What an amazing feeling to be alone in Central Park and still be surrounded by millions of invisible people. It was a balmy night, a little like spring, you could smell the ground defrosting."

She paused to surrender to memory. Phil scratched at the back of his neck. The rash on his face was a violent red. Quickly I reminded Rita to tell us exactly what happened.

*

"It all started," she said, "with that play I went to see last night. It was one of those Theatre of the Absurd plays, called *In the Full Light of Emptiness*. The theme was about a kind of predestination based on the immutability of an individual's essential nature. There were five actors—three men and two women—fastened to five slowly rotating wheels. Every time one of the wheels stopped, the actor on it would play out his part in the drama. The playwright, of course was permitting them to live out the illusion of self-determination, but the audience knew that no matter what each one said or did, he would go round and round, forever in his own orbit, merely re-enacting what he had been doing all his life. There were many changes of scene, but nothing really happened. Very complex. Brilliant piece of writing.

"You know these plays? Right from the start you get caught up in some bizarre situation. There are no throw-away lines: every word counts. So I was annoyed when a man comes in late, after the curtain goes up. He takes the seat beside me, then begins to fuss with his overcoat, then fumbles with a paper bag and unwraps a sandwich. 'My dinner,' he says to me, because by this time I'm watching *his* act. After a while, just when I'm concentrating on some poignant lines, he starts on a package of gum and chews furiously. At the beginning of the second act, the same business again: the curtain goes up and he becomes restless. He searches through his suit pockets, then the coat pockets, for more gum, I suppose. He must have run out, because he starts chewing his nails. I knew how he felt—everyone in that audience was going through his own total recall. My hands were clenched; he was gnawing at his. 'Elliott,' I turned to him, 'stop biting your nails.' And I reached out and he gave me his hand, and I simply held it to keep him from chewing it off. You remember Elliott Benson, Sophie? I used to have to hold his hand in the movies. Anyway, all that business in the play where reality is an illusion and self-deception is the truth; and there is no distinction between the true and the false; where fantasy and fact are indistinguishable—it all reached a point at the end of the second act when I no longer knew anything. It was as if knowing and not knowing were the same state. You don't get it? Never mind.

"We went out together at the second intermission. He did look a little like my Elliott—the same height and colouring. He was a man of about fifty, as Elliott would be now. He was an odd person in a way. He wore an old-fashioned double-breasted suit, yet his hair was cut in a joe-college crew cut. He grinned like a kid, but had deep creases in his face that made him look old and weary. He said,

'I waited last night in the usual place, but you didn't show.'

'My father wouldn't let me see you again,' I told him.

'I stayed as long as I could, then I had to leave.'

'You should have waited for me. If you had waited, just a little longer, I would have gone with you. Poppa had to weaken some time.'

'Is your father dead?'

'I'm not sure.'

"In the last act, all the characters in the play were left suspended in limbo, immobilized forever by their own natures. Elliott and I left the theatre together.

'Not much point in going on,' I said.

'It's not a question of choice,' he replied.

"We walked, without speaking. We were now actually on Fifth Avenue, yet in a mysterious way we were out of context with place and time.

'Where would you like to stop on your wheel?' he asked.

'In Weyburn, Saskatchewan. Circa 1938.'

'I don't wish to be ungallant,' he said, 'but if that's the case, then it is still the Depression and we have absolutely no money. We shall have to keep walking.'

"Do you know, it is quite a marvelous feeling to be young again and free, free even of money. When we came to the park, we ran and raced along until I had no breath left. We found a bench and continued our make-believe in the manner of small children.

'You,' he said, 'must be Helen.'

'Of course. That's only fair, if you are Elliott.'

'And I must work in your father's drug store.'

'And I must feel sorry for you, because you are very intelligent and yet my father won't trust you to do anything but sweep the store and deliver orders.'

'You begin to hang around the store and your father fires me.'

'Then we must meet secretly in the park behind the school.'

"And so we reconstructed a probable past, shaping it with the materials of a possible future that had long since disappeared into eternity. It is the Everest of desire, this sort of wish fulfillment. You are on the mountain-top without an oxygen mask and you feel as if something inside will burst any minute. Yet there you are and the view is irresistible. We kept switching from the real self to the person who might have been in relation to the other. Poor man's Pirandello, you might say.

"At sunrise, we were still the star-crossed lovers, wandering from bench to bench. We were now in the midst of the Second World War. Elliott had been wounded and discharged home. I had gone East to Toronto. My father would not give Elliott my address.

'I know someone who will tell you where to find me. Sophie's mother,' I told him.

'And where do I find you?'

'In Toronto. I have the unhappy job of typing two thousand envelopes a day for a mail order firm.'

'I shall never forget it,' he said, 'your indifference when I show up at your rooming house. I sit on the edge of a chair like some insurance salesman. We are strangers. You try to be polite, but I have the feeling you are in a hurry, and I'm holding you back from something very important.'

'Surely I am still in love with you,' I insisted.

'You couldn't be; you are Helen.'

'It is possible. I have made many mistakes.'

'Perhaps it is just as well you spurn me; I become ambitious.'

'Must I reject you?'

'Yes. It is my fate. All women, even my wife, start out as Helen and become strangers.'

'Now you be my Elliott. You must believe in me. Be patient; wait for me.'

'All right. As Elliott I persevere. I do not give you up. Then the pursuit of love absorbs me entirely. I remain the errand boy. You understand that, don't you? A man cannot give himself over to a woman completely and at the same time succeed in the world. Eventually he is forced to choose.'

'The lady or the tiger?'

'That's about it. I have a tiger by the tail. It is a man-eating corporation, with thirty thousand people running errands for me over the entire globe. Now, suppose I had taken the lady...' "

Rita stopped.

"Then what happened?" I asked.

"Nothing happened." Rita replied. "We found our way out of the park. Elliott put me into a cab and said he would call me later today. The only thing that *happened* was the writing of the phone number—yours. You look cynical. You needn't be. By the way, if you answer, remember he will ask for Helen. We never did reveal our true names."

Phil said, "I don't think you should see him again."

"Why not?" Rita asked. "There's no harm in it."

"You had your fun. Let it go at that. You know as well as I that men don't play games forever. Neither of you will be satisfied with pretense for very long."

"I've been trying to tell you our charade was very serious. In a way, we were going through a kind of reincarnation. I must find out where I went wrong the first time and what I might have done with a second chance. I must see Elliott again."

"You're as absurd as those crazy plays. This nonsense will lead to trouble. A pick-up is a pick-up. He'll go along with the gag, of course, what has he to lose? But you'll have to carry on your affair from some other base. I will not assist in your debauchery."

"Phil, you must trust me, I'll do nothing wrong!"

Rita turned to me with a look that begged intervention. All this time I had been listening to her with a degree of sympathy: her story was a version of the tales told in my mother's kitchen—of lovers in the moonlight at the river's edge, who meet, and sigh, and part forever. Phil, too, sought my attention, demanding loyalty to him. His reaction was understandable: no man trusts the motives of his own sex. I got up from the table and began to wash dishes. I can think better when my hands are busy. In the silence I longed for the sound of music, but I clattered plates instead.

When the telephone rang, I was putting the dishes away in the cupboard. Rita and Phil simultaneously sprang to answer it. Phil got to the hall first. As she jumped up, Rita's head struck the edge of the open cupboard door. These old cupboards are made of solid, heavy wood, and the impact must have been stunning. She staggered for a moment, then kept going. I could see her in the hall, clutching the side of her head and groping blindly for the phone with the other hand. Phil held the instrument high, out of her reach. He was saying, "Hello. Yes. No, there is no one here with that name. I'm quite certain. Yes, that is the number, but there is no one here named Helen."

We all heard the click as the caller hung up. Phil's hand was still upraised with the instrument in it, when Rita suddenly cradled her head in her arms. She pressed against the wall, she slid down, doubled over, and passed out.

*

The doctor didn't think there was any concussion and advised observation. Her pulse, he thought, was a bit rapid, she should stay in bed for a day, just to calm her down a bit. I sat by Rita's bed the rest of the evening. What did the doctor mean calm her down? She lay perfectly still, her head turned away from me. Just once she spoke,

"Oh, Sophie, I shall never find out what became of me."

THE MEANS

On the Paris-Marseilles train I sat with my forehead pressed against the glass, eyes unblinking, hands tightly clasped, in anticipation—of what? I cannot understand my yearning to get on this train for an eight hour trip when the plane gets me there in an hour. Back home, I explained, "I am going to follow the route traversed by Vincent van Gogh, whom I have admired ever since I purchased a print of *Sunflowers* when I was sixteen. For twenty-seven years, I have been obsessed with the life and art of one of the greatest painters of our century. It is my hope to experience what he must have felt when he turned his back on the grey skies of Paris for the blinding light of the Midi." (I speak in this documentary fashion to cover a confusion. My listener is intimidated by such pedantry and quickly switches to a topic less likely to elicit unprofitable discourse—switches to, say, the decline in the quality of the cuisine aboard aircraft. Otherwise, a dialogue would not be possible.)

There were six of us in the compartment, sitting knee to knee. Obliquely across from me was a middle-aged lady, with a fine, sharp nose and brooding eyes, red hair drawn tight and braids across the top of her head, looking exactly like van Gogh's *La Berceuse*. Her broad hips took up one half of the seat, causing two men, strangers to one another, to crowd self-consciously into the other half. In her hands she held loosely the ties of a string bag, instead, as in the painting, the cords of a cradle. It was an omen, I felt. Perhaps I was fulfilling a prophecy made by a fortune teller when I was eighteen, that same year I sailed alone to see a father I didn't remember. I recall Masquerade Night aboard that ocean liner. I came dressed as *L'Arlesienne*, using a white slip for my shawl and a white dining-room napkin for my cap. No one recognized the source of the costume. The "gypsy" held my hands, palms up, and said, "You will take a long train journey. I hear a train whistle." I was awed by her omniscience: How could she know I was going to my father in Marseilles? (Actually everyone took the boat-train from Cherbourg to Paris.) "Am I going to be happy?" I asked her. She looked up into my eyes, turned my hands over and patted them. I demanded to know: "Am I going to be happy?" "Of course," she said, "but not right away."

Today, twenty-five years later, I was happy to sit on that train again. I found that the grey of Paris did indeed change to blinding light. By standards of Canadian distances, this happened quickly. The skies became bluer, the light more brilliant. It was early May and the fields lay open to the sun. Trees were showing their first tender green; fruit trees were in blossom. Renewal everywhere. Across the ledges of second-storey windows were flung the red comforters of winter, spread to air in the spring sun. The exact red of van Gogh's blanket in *Bedroom at Arles*. Then miles of vineyards with little vines close to the earth. An excitement rose: I could feel Vincent's resurgence of hope as he approached his destination. The change in the light would bring a change in fortune. The bleak past would vanish. The hot sun of the Midi would ease his tortured spirit. Finally, glimpses of the Mediterranean, his blue sea; and beside the railroad tracks, (his) wild irises in that joyous purple-blue. My eyes were so full of bright pictures that I couldn't see clearly when the train pulled into the station at Marseilles. As I descended from the train, suitcase in hand, I lingered on the second step to adjust my vision. Little dark people scurried in all directions, food carts getting in the way of porters' trucks. And all bathed in an eerie green light that came from a glassed-in dome, high overhead. Hollow voices echoed in a canyon. Between me and what I saw and heard, was an infinite distance I could never bridge. I stood paralyzed. Then, in panic, I turned around to go back up to the train compartment. My path was blocked by a small line of people waiting for me to step down out of their way. The conductor was holding out a helping hand. I missed his hand, as well as the bottom step, and went sprawling. My head hit the iron wheel of a baggage truck. Now I could close my eyes. I welcomed the pain in my head. Just before I passed out, I noted to myself that pain has to be physical to be bearable. Or else why would Vincent have cut off an ear, if not to displace his soul's anguish to a spot he could touch?

I felt a cold, wet cloth being pressed against my forehead. A murmur of voices. I caught the words doctor and hospital. I looked up at La Berceuse, whose large breasts blocked my view of everything else. *"Pas de docteur. Je doit aller à Arles!"* My head was pillowed on my suitcase, purse rested on my stomach. I grinned wildly, repeating my determination to take the next train to Arles. I thought I was speaking French. No one paid attention. This came as a surprise. That terrible time with my father did teach me, at the very least, to speak a decent French. I reached into my purse, found my pen and notebook, and printed in large shaky letters, ARLES. "Ah," they chorused, "Arles . . . " But it sounded different.

An hour later I stood, as perhaps Vincent did, in the last light outside the little station house in Arles. In the empty yard, a taxi. After that *débâcle* in the Saint-Charles Station, I no longer trusted my accent. I printed in my notebook, "Hôtel Nord-Pinu," tore out the page and held it before the driver's eyes.

No one was at the hotel desk. Walls and worn carpets and big stuffed furniture were giving off that strong soap and mildew smell which belongs to interiors with a respected past. Nowhere had I read that van Gogh was ever inside such a hotel. He was a guest only in an insane asylum. Standing there I ruminated on the countless persons who had sought the sun of the Midi, who had come and gone in this hotel, unaware of the genius painting in the square outside. Possibly, if they did come upon him at his easel, they mocked his work. I felt a profound outrage. I would not stay here.

The motel off the *Place du Forum*, called the *Hôtel du Forum*, was of the same vintage as its neighbour and had the same odours. I was led through endless halls, barely lit. "Two steps down, one step up, three steps down." Visible on the walls were prints of Renoir, Cézanne, Lautrec, Braque, Gauguin. No van Goghs. Perhaps in revenge for not having been immortalized like its twin hotel next door. Into a large shuttered room. *"Ouvrez la fenêtre, s'il vous plait,"* I asked. The motherly, cheery woman did not understand. I had a hard time with the heavy bolts and hinges after she hurried out. The gesture of (violently) flinging open the windows recalled the bitter quarrels with my father, all in fluent French, regarding his insistence on closed, shuttered windows.

Early the next morning I set out to pay homage to Vincent van Gogh. In the squares were generals on horseback. In the shops, van Gogh shared space with postcards of Roman ruins. In the Tourist Bureau, reproductions in cardboard boxes on a small table in a corner farthest from t.

door. In the *Musée de Rattée* not a single van Gogh. Two memorials only: in the little park a bust of him, donated by its sculptor; on a street corner, high up against a telephone pole, a sign with an arrow pointing to the Vincent van Gogh Hospital. Tourists everywhere, filing into medieval churches with heads bowed; standing respectfully in the Roman amphitheatre. Vincent was indifferent to antiquity, and antiquity has prevailed.

Each day I wandered the streets. I was drawn to follow the narrow old streets to the bottom of town. I stepped aside for the young men and women rushing off to work in the morning; shopkeepers held their brooms until I passed; motorcycles came roaring out of nowhere, forcing me to flatten myself against cold walls. Finally, I would reach the river, where it was quiet, except for a monstrous dredging machine dripping mud from its jaws, pounding out a monotonous beat. I walked along the cement retaining wall, avoiding dog shit, gazing at the sluggish, muddy waters of the Rhône, trying to imagine the blue of *On the Banks of the Rhône*. The banks of the Rhône were piled high with garbage, despite the *"Défense de —"* signs. Once I watched two thin ladies in black carrying household *débris* in heavy armfuls and throwing it over the wall. They spent an entire morning this way, going back and forth from some dark, smelly hole of a house (I imagined) clearing out the remains of someone else's life. It was as if their determination to toss into the river cartons of dirt and old plaster, two soiled, flat mattresses, broken dishes and bent pots, was going to give them a new start. Perhaps it did. Behind me, straining from the pocked walls of an abandoned *préfecture*, a pair of ancient caryatids looked down on a pair of Esso gas pumps. Only Vincent's golden disc floated effulgent in a benign blue sky.

At noon, the shops are closed, the café tables on the sidewalks empty, my room in darkness. I fling open the shutters after a struggle.

"Damn you!" I shout at some middle-aged woman who has bent a rounded back over my bed; at some widow who has arranged clean towels; at, perhaps, an abandoned mother of six who has mopped the tile floor, "Idiot! Don't you know there is only the light, nothing but light to warm us!"

The room is dank. I lie shivering on top of the red feather comforter, in a fever of doubt. It has all been to no avail. What have cornfields and fishing boats and the Postmaster Roulin to do with me? I have lost a connection. The world of van Gogh does not exist. I only imagined it. Everywhere the stench of cars and trucks; everywhere busloads of tourists in dark glasses; everywhere servants and shopkeepers, who say *merci, madame* and do not look at me. For a moment I know the nature of failure: not a drop of pity anywhere. I am the beggar at the sight of whom people cross the street. I am desolate. I am also hungry.

The little restaurant off the square is crowded. The owner (I think she is, from her officious manner) leads me to the only empty seat, opposite a young man. He wears a heavy, dark business suit in a roomful of jeans and jerseys. The skin on his hands is red with scratches, and the nails, cut close, are black-edged. His face is ten years younger than his hands. A heavy, blunt reality about him, like van Gogh's Dutch peasants. He and I are the only ones with cropped hair. While I pretend to read the menu, I notice his white shirt has irreparable creases ironed into the edges of the collar and cuffs. No matter how I try, I also iron the selfsame creases into the same places. I feel a bond with the shirt-ironers of the world. I order fish and a small bottle of white wine. She does not have small bottles of white wine. Just large ones like *M'sieu's*. I decline. Does he intend to polish off all that wine by himself, I wonder. I eat my salad and *pâté*, looking up at my companion every time I raise my fork. His rounded forehead glistens. He keeps his eyes on what he is eating, follows each forkful of *blanquette de veau* on its way to his mouth, his eyes almost crossed at the finish. He chews self-consciously, drinks his wine steadily. I don't mind the silence between us: My marriage has prepared me for eating with strangers. I know from experience that, should I desire conversation, it is up to me to start to chatter, to ask proper questions. On the other hand, perhaps a faulty French would be better than no words at all. Again, I recalled that my command of the language had been sufficient for long arguments as to whether, at eighteen, I was old enough to be out alone on the streets of Marseilles. I stare at the stranger across the table, my mind searching for a name to go with his (familiar) face.

The owner-waitress returns and swings her long, blonde (bleached) hair at us. She, too, wears jeans and a jersey, although she is neither young nor slim.

"Is everything all right?" she asks me in English.

"Fine, everything is just fine."

My companion addresses her in a rapid speech, with the seriousness of a defence lawyer. She nods agreement, and pours wine from his bottle into my glass.

"*Merci beaucoup,*" I say to him.

We continue to eat and drink thoughtfully. I approach my fish, and he is into his strawberries. The next time I look up, he asks, wordlessly, holding the bottle over my emptied glass, if I would like some more wine.

"*Oui, s'il vous plait.*"

He fills the glass.

"*Merci beaucoup.*"

"You are very welcome indeed," he replies. In English. The bones in my fish are tiny and I exercise great care.

A small victory, his. I don't mind: I'm accustomed to small defeats. He stands up. With a final flourish, he pours the remainder of the wine into my glass. Picks up an attaché case, inclines his head and leaves. I feel an old (silent) rage at being abandoned. I throw thirty francs on the table and run out after him.

He is the only figure in the square. The night is navy blue, like *Starry Night*, with the same big, yellow stars. I touch his sleeve and he pulls away. I take hold of the rough wool.

"It is not enough to share the wine," I tell him, "a few kind words to go with a kind act . . . "

"Madame . . . ?"

He is waiting for me to reveal a cause, a plan, a purpose. I have none. At the same time, I know *he* is the cause, the plan, the purpose. In what way, I must find out.

"Please, I must talk to someone—must talk to you."

I sense his reluctance, but he follows me just the same, across the square, to the hotel. Inside, I lead down the dark halls, "two steps down, one step up, three steps down." Tonight, I am glad the lights in my room are so dim. Neither of us knows my intention. We sit facing each other at a card table in the middle of the room. I bring a small bottle of brandy and the only glass from the bathroom. We take turns sipping from the glass. His elbows are on the table, thick knuckles against his cheeks, round brown eyes steady. There is a tacit agreement to take our time.

"Madame was surprised to my English, *non?*"

"One surprise led to another, *non?*"

"*Touché!* So pleasant . . . "

"You may lose sleep . . . "

"But yes," with both hands in the air, "I have all of eternity for sleep . . . "

I watch him closely. I feel I am on the verge of some

knowledge: something more than my implied invitation bargained for. It comes when he leans forward and smiles, in a manner that mixes desire and diffidence. From the very first, everything about this man reminded me of the boy I met in a café on a hot afternoon in Marseilles twenty-five years ago. Now he is telling me about himself.

"I also speak German, Italian and Spanish; it is necessary to my work. I am returning from a three-week study of Provence. I, who was born in Saint-Victoir! Regard my hands: I must help my parents with the grapes. Tomorrow I study Arles. The tourists want more than scenery. It is necessary, n'est-ce pas, to inform oneself from time to time, or one loses the enthusiasm?"

In the lapel of his jacket, which he is still wearing, buttoned to the top, even though I have kicked off my shoes as a first gesture—in the lapel he holds towards me is a white and green enamel pin. "I am a member of the Association for Professional Guides." Returning the courtesy, I show him my passport. He does not take it right away.

"It is not necessary," he says, "I have been a guide for ten years and one learns one's way with all sorts."

I must assume that by "all sorts" he does not intend deprecation. All the same, he is turning the pages slowly.

"Born in Austria . . . ," he murmurs. Then, "Not many ladies travel alone . . . what brings madame to Arles, if you will pardon me."

"I have long admired the work of Vincent van Gogh. I have come to Provence to pay homage to a man whose life was so tragic and whose work was so great." Again, my archaic speech in a flat voice leaves my listener bewildered.

"Madame paints?"

"No, I no longer paint." My bravado is evaporating. "And my name is Margaret." Help me, I silently plead with him. . . . Silently, he returns my passport. . . .

"Where do you live?" I ask dramatically, as if inspired.
"In Marseilles, in a terrible apartment. My wife lives
mostly at the doctor's . . . "

He has removed his jacket, but it is in order to find
something. He hands me a leather case.

I assure him, "It is not necessary, I am old enough to
know what I'm doing." Just the same I fumble with the case,
three cards fall out onto the table, one of them is his birth
certificate, which I study. He is thirty-four years old, born
in Saint-Victoir, as he said. His surname is not the one I
remember.

"Forgive me, Marguerite"—my name in his mouth becomes romantic—"do not misunderstand me, but what has
your journey to do with me?"

If he is so experienced with "all sorts" can't he see I am
equally puzzled by my conduct? He stands before me, his
jacket over his arm, impatient, the way he would with a
straggler who needs to be urged to get onto the waiting
bus with its motor running.

I take his jacket, drape it over his chair.

"Please," I say, "can't you see . . . the advantage is yours
. . . "

It wasn't difficult, after all. In bed he dealt with me at
first with the deference-disdain as in the restaurant. I
opened to him. I found I wanted to give all I possibly could.
His manner went from self-control, to laughter, to a passion
that bordered on violence. Towards the end, we lost all
strangeness. And finished off with wild kisses.

Sitting up, legs touching, desultory jokes in a whisper
about French cooking *à la campagne*, about tourists, about
cheap wine. He keeps calling me Marguerite. He relates a
funny story about de Gaulle. I cannot bring myself to speak
his name, lest I pronounce the one pounding in my head,
Raoul. He shifts about and yawns and yawns. Why does

he not give way to sleep? I interpret this as the Samson syndrome: He is waiting for Delilah's betrayal. I do not wish to deceive him.

"You remind me of someone I met twenty-five years ago."

"Is that why you wanted me, simply that I look like another?"

"No, no, more than that. I fainted at the Saint-Charles Station. The skylight, van Gogh, your face—they are all mixed up with a terrible experience when I was a young girl. I'm afraid to go back alone to the station."

"You wish for me to accompany you to Marseilles?"

"And stay with me until I leave for the airport. Would you do that?"

"But of course."

On the train in the morning he listens to me, his round head to one side, his fingers spread out on his knees. His eyes on me unwavering.

"As you saw, I was born in Austria. When the war came, my father deserted my mother and me because my mother is Jewish. He wasn't. We survived somehow. No thanks to him. After the war my uncle brought us to Toronto. In the winter of 1948, I traced my father to France. I wrote him; he replied, yes he would like to see his daughter. My mother was upset. She asked me to be absolutely certain I wanted to know a father who abandoned his family to the Nazis. In the spring I sailed to Cherbourg, took the train to Marseilles. I had illusions of setting up an easel in the *Place du Forum* in Arles, my father would sit at a sidewalk table café in that picture and he would be proud of me. My unhappy existence would flower into a rich and satisfying life. Nothing like that happened. The first disappointment for us both was regarding money: He thought *I* was wealthy and I thought *he* was wealthy. We were penniless.

I paid for our first meal with a few dollars left over from the trip. For the three months I stayed with him we fought constantly."

When we come to the outskirts of Marseilles, my friend (he is now) points to blocks of apartments, gray even in sunlight, and says one of those small windows is his.

Suddenly, we are in semi-darkness. We have arrived at the Saint-Charles Station. I do not want to leave my seat. After everyone has left the coach, he takes me by the hand. We step down together onto the platform. I look up at that skylight and down again: I cannot absorb the scene: Men and women and children, vendors and porters, kiosks and restaurants; strange forms melting into one another under that greenish light. My hand in his is wet. I hide my face against his sleeve. He stands absolutely still.

When I open my eyes, I find I am in the middle of a large European railway station. Under the clear light of a glassed-in dome, high overhead, there are men, women and children, porters and food vendors. It is a typical Latin scene, colourful and exciting. There is a cheerful clatter. We sit down in the restaurant. I want a cognac. Two. I laugh with relief. He looks triumphant, almost.

Out into the sunlight, down broad stairs on which a miniature city disports itself. Pedestrians rushing up and down the steps; little cafés at the sides; everywhere hustlers of quick pleasures. At ten in the morning the heat is portentous. The fruit in the stands is beginning to spoil: Oranges give off a sweet, rotten odour. I have been down these stairs before. The Basques are still here, gaunt and worried, waiting, sitting on their rolled-up carpets, loaves of bread close by. At the bottom of the stairs, on either side, I recognize the monstrous, arrogant monuments looking down, in the acute sense of the words, on the ancient town below. When we come to the tree-shaded avenue, I take the lead. A right turn into the *Rue de la Saunerie*, which is more like an alley than a street. An open sewer runs in the gutter. Around us, the very stones stink.

"Here, at Number 26, on the second floor, in two rooms. I slept in my father's bed and he on the kitchen floor. Sometimes he brought a woman, never the same one twice. I was not allowed to go out alone. One afternoon, when he was using the bed, I sneaked out. This way, down this street, *La Canebière*, I remember it very well now, I walked and walked, looking in shop windows, it was a glorious day, I was happy to be free."

Within sight of the Old Port, my companion halts at a corner. He removes my arm from within his. He leans back against a wall, pale, his big eyes narrowed.

"I am expected at home," he says, "I live quite a distance from here, and I must say *au 'voir*. A taxi will take you back to the station. Here is your baggage claim. There's a bus to the airport from Saint-Charles."

The (hidden) purpose that caused me to run after this man last night is still operating.

"Come along, hurry, we're almost there." We come to a café; I fall into the nearest chair. "Here, here is where I stopped."

He stands there, on one foot, so to speak.

"We are five minutes from the *Parc du Pharo*, where you can enjoy a rest and an interesting panorama. I must go now."

"Sit down!" My voice peremptory. Have I ceased to beg? "Anyway, in this café, a young man came to my table, apologized, asked if I was American, I said I was Canadian, no matter, he wanted to have English conversation, was the way he put it, since it would help him in his studies. His name was Raoul. You could be his brother. He bought me an ice. Two. We talked. He said he liked coming to this part of the city to observe life. We agreed to meet, same place, same time, the next day. I never saw him again. That's all. Now, I want an ice. Two."

"I am in his place?"

"Yes."

"And last night—the same?"

"Yes. Forgive me. We all pay a price. My husband and my sons think I am strong. They leave me alone. I have no one. You must stay."

Without pride I am a poor adversary. Without a contest, without loss or gain, he probably feels he is wasting his time. I sense his disappointment.

He tells me, "There is no mystery about you after all."

We walk under the merciless sun, past the poor fishermen and their boats; past the rich men and their yachts. Past the *Parc du Pharo*, past *Fort Saint-Nicholas*, where a young guard stands with glazed eyes, his khaki shirt soaked in sweat. We should walk on the other, the shaded side, my companion suggests, but I am determined to sweat it out, as I did once before. Uphill all the way. He drags his jacket, mops his forehead. When we come to the *corniche* overlooking the Mediterranean, we stop to stare at the blue sea.

"It was night," I went on, "when I got home. My father was sitting at the kitchen table, facing the door, looking dark and stern. 'Like mother, like daughter.' There was a terrible scene: I had disobeyed him. He said he could imagine what my mother had done to stay alive—whore that she was. As for me, he was going to keep me decent. He locked me in the apartment, closed the shutters. It was summer: two months of hell. One night in my sleep I went after him with a big kitchen knife. The next morning he told me I was to leave. Once outside, he began walking along this very same route, carrying my suitcase, away from the Saint-Charles railway station. Where he taking me? I followed obediently, torn between joy in my freedom and fear of his intentions. When we came to this look-out, right here, beside the wall, he began to shout abuses at me. I hung my head: don't anger him now, I told myself, you will soon escape him. As calmly as I could, I reached for my suitcase. At that precise moment, he lifted it high with both hands, and with all his strength threw it. I watched my suitcase in the air briefly, a black square against the blue sea, saw it hit the water, float for a bit, then a wave submerged it. The waters closed over everything I owned, including my passport and my return boat ticket."

My friend did not press me to continue. I don't know how long I stood there, paralyzed by memory. Silent, unmoving, he stood between me and the sea. Then he held me until I stopped trembling. All at once I was overcome by a terrible fatigue, similar to that following childbirth. I was weary and spent.

"If you are anxious to go on," I said, "I'll take a taxi back. I think I'll rest here for a while."

"I have served my purpose?"

"It was not planned that way."

"I understand . . . "

"I know. Thank you. You have helped me . . . "

"No, no Marguerite, the sympathy is for your father. It is *he* I understand, I understand what was the necessity for him. You . . . you . . . ," The round head was shaking from side to side, "you go against the circumstance."

"My father," I whispered, "was angry because I did not get on my knees. Is that what you mean?"

"No . . . yes . . . to have lost a daughter, to have suffered much, certainly to have the guilt, then . . . a miracle! You appear. To forgive, perhaps. But no. You have not an interest in him, it is the adventure you wish. He punishes you. For what it is I do not know: perhaps it is the disappointment." He put his face closer to mine. "You appear the weak one, the lost one, but at the bottom you are made of iron. It is confusing. It angers one not to know, perhaps to have made a mistake. Since yesterday I often have the desire to finish the masquerade."

"What am I to do? I intend no harm. I suffer more than anyone."

"I too have been reading about van Gogh. He was speaking quietly, his face close to mine. "Even a diseased prostitute knew better than to trust her life to him. And the saintly Theo, he died feeling guilty. Van Gogh knew what he wanted, and what he wanted was at odds with circumstances. You are like that."

"There is no comparison, he was unique, he was a genius . . . !"

"You must see . . . do you not see . . . this is how it is . . . ," I was startled by his agitation. "If I leave you here now, alone and lost, I, too, will suffer the guilt. I did not seek the circumstance of your necessity, but I must be honorable."

"Go! I'll find my way back."

"*Exactement.*"

I laughed. "I'm surprised I had the wit to pursue you. It's all so clear—so simple really. . . . "

At the Terminus Hotel, next to the Saint-Charles Station, we made telephone calls from our room. He to say he had been delayed, and I to cancel my flight. We talked a good deal about ourselves. I recovered much of my former fluency in French. I was elated, found everything very funny, threw myself about on the bed. I spent my exuberance on his body. His passivity should have been a warning. As the first light appeared at the window, I dropped off to sleep. I had been asleep a few minutes (an hour?) when I felt or heard something. I opened my eyes. He was sitting on the edge of the bed, fully dressed, his jacket buttoned. I reached for his hand.

"Why . . . ?"

"Never did you call me by name . . . all night long . . . if you had spoken my name once . . . if only once . . . "

It was true. Desperately, I pictured his birth certificate and searched for the print, but could only visualize the date.

"I do not exist for you," he went on, "you set out to put an end to something and I was the means. Adieu, madame."

Later that morning I was on the express train to Paris. The countryside was still burgeoning with Spring, but it had nothing to do with anything or anyone in particular.

MY MOTHER'S LUCK

July 6, 1931

I have decided, my mother said, to go with you to New York to see you off. Your boat sails a week from tomorrow. In a week you will be gone; who knows if we will ever see each other again. No, no, stop it. I can't stand anyone slobbering over me. *Now* what are you crying for? I thought you wanted to go to your father. I'm only trying to do what's best for you. You should be happy, going to Europe, to Germany, travelling in style, like a tourist. Not the way we came to this country, eh? Steerage, like cattle. Everything on that boat smelled and tasted of oily ropes. Hardly what you would call a pleasure trip. But then, how would I recognize pleasure—how would I know what there is in this world that gives happiness—when I have been working since I was nine years old. My feet, my poor feet. I can't remember when my feet didn't hurt. Get me the white basin, no, the deep one, from under the sink. And the kettle: the water should be hot enough. Take a chair, sit down. No, I'll fill it myself. We will have a talk while I'm soaking my feet. I suppose we should have a talk before you go. I know, I know; you don't have to remind me; can I help it, the long hours; you think I like to work so hard? It's not only you I have no time for: I don't have time to breathe, to live. I said, sit down! What do you care about your silly girl friends? They'll find someone else to waste their time with. Jennie? Write her a letter. Ah, that feels better. My poor feet. I'm looking forward to sitting on the train. They told me it takes fourteen hours from Toronto to New York. Just think, I will be off my feet for a whole day.

Why do you look so miserable? I just don't understand you: first you drive me crazy to go to your father and now you sit like at a funeral. Tell you what: in New York we will have a little party before your boat sails. We'll go to a big, fancy restaurant. Sam and me and you. Yes. You heard right. Sam. Are you deaf or don't you understand Yiddish any more? I said, Sam is coming with us. You might as well know: he is moving in with me next week. Your room. No use leaving it empty. There you go again, telling me what I should do. No one tells me what to do. I will stay alone until the Messiah comes, rather than live with another woman. I despise women: they are false and jealous. With a man you know where you're at: you either get along or you don't. They are not hypocrites like women. Marry Sam? What for? To give satisfaction to the old *yentes*, the gossips? I will never marry again: three times was plenty. Get a little hot water from the kettle. Ah, that's better. Now turn low the gas.

So, tell me, have you got your underwear and stockings clean for the trip? Your shoes need a good polish. You don't need everything new. Let your father buy you something, I've supported you for sixteen years, that's long enough. God knows as He is my witness I can do no more. That's what I told your teacher when she came to see me in the winter. She looked around the flat as if fish was rotting under her nose. I couldn't wait for her to leave, that dried up old maid. I told her, I'm an ignorant woman, I'll let you educated people figure out what to do with my daughter. Just one thing you should remember, Esther, it was your idea, not mine, that you should get in touch with your father. Whatever happens, you will not be able to blame

me. Of course, you can come back if you want. You have
a return ticket. You can thank Sam for that. He said I should
let you make up your own mind if you want to live with
your father. You don't deserve Sam's consideration. The
way you treat him: not talking to him when he greets you
on his Sunday visits. He—what? Watch that tongue of
yours. I can still give you a good licking if I have to. The
smell of sweat is the smell of honest work. I don't like it
either, but I've had enough from the educated ones, like
your father, who know everything except how to raise a
sweat. They all talked a lot, but I could never find out what
they wanted from me. I cooked and cleaned and went to
work. I tried to please the customers all day and then I was
supposed to please them at night.

Like that talmudist, Avrom, you remember him—well,
perhaps you were too young. One night I came home from
work, tired and hungry, and there he was, exactly where
I had left him at eight o'clock in the morning, at the kitchen
table. In twelve hours nothing had changed, except there
were more books and more dirty plates on the table. —And
where, I asked him, am I supposed to eat? He didn't even
look up. He raised a white hand. —What means the hand
in the air? You think maybe this is Poland and you are the
privileged scholar, the permanent guest at my table? In
America everybody works who wants to eat. With my arm,
like with a broom, I swept clear the table. I waited he should
say something, maybe he would realize and say he was
sorry he forgot about me, but all he did was look at me
like he didn't know who I was. Then he bent down and
picked up the books one by one, so slow you would think
every book weighed a ton. His face got red like his hair,
he was breathing so noisy I thought he was going to bust.
Just the books, not the dishes, he picked up. He went into
the bedroom and closed the door. All I asked was a little
consideration, and for that he didn't talk to me for a week.

So what's the difference to me whether they know enough to take a bath. Sam will learn. He needs a nice home. He's a good man, he works hard, a presser in a factory. So maybe he will be tired at night. And he can pay his own way to New York. A working man has at least his union to see he gets a decent wage. What protection has a scholar got? He leans on the whole world and the world pushes him away. Not that I care about money. I am decent with a man, not taking from him every cent, like their greedy wives. Last week Sam handed me his sealed pay envelope. —Here, he said, take out for New York. Buy yourself a nice coat. Naturally, I wouldn't take his money. So long as he pays the rent, a little for the food, it will be enough. If I was to take his money, next thing he will be telling me what I should do. You can be sure the minute he tries to boss me, out he goes, like the others.

Your step-father, the first one, made that mistake. Max. Tall, the best looking man I ever knew. He worked all night in a bakery and came home seven o'clock in the morning smelling like fresh bread. You two got along well. He made you lunch every day and filled your pockets with bagels for your class. Every Saturday he took you to the show. Remember? When I came home from the store Saturday night, which was his night off, he was ready to step out. I could only soak my tired feet. One day he got a raise. —Lily, he said, you can stop work. Sell the store. Stay home and look after Esther and me. I said, —and suppose you lost your job, what will become of us in this Depression? And suppose your boss gives your job to his brother who came last night from Poland? Max thought we should take a chance. —Maybe someday I will have my own bakery, he said, I want you should stay home like a normal wife. He was not very intelligent: he couldn't get it into his head we would have no security without my beauty parlor. After that, Max was not the same. He talked to me as if I was his servant. —You, he would call me, instead of my name; you, don't make me nothing to eat. I have a bad stomach. —See a doctor. —A doctor won't help. I choke on your meat. He came and went in his work clothes, so that there was flour dust on the furniture. I even paid for the lawyer to get the divorce, just to get rid of him.

What are you sitting like a lump for? Get me a little hot water in the basin. Careful, slow, do you want to burn me! You are such a *shlimazel!* Wipe it up. Are you blind as well? There, over there, by the stove. Ah, that feels good. I hope you will have it easier than me. Maybe your father can give you the education your teacher said you should have. All I have from life is sore feet. My poor feet, look how cal-loused and shapeless they have become. Once I had such fine hands and feet. The ankles, they used to be so thin. When I was young they said I had the hands and feet of an aristocrat. If you're really so smart as they say you are, you won't have to slave like me. You should have a life like the aristocrats in Europe used to have before the Rev-olution. I hope you will have a name everyone respects. What a life those fine ladies of Europe used to have: they got married and lived free as birds. Like George Sand or Madame de Staël. Surprised you, eh? I know more than you think. In the papers I recognize names sometimes I first hear in Zürich: Freud, Einstein, Picasso. What's the matter? See, I did learn something from your father. He may tell you I was stupid, he used to tell me I was an ignorant ghetto girl.

Your father taught me to read and write in German. He tried to educate me. So did Isaac. I could always tell there was going to be trouble when they said—Lily, try and un-derstand . . . And then I'd get a lecture. You would think that after your father I would not again be trapped by fine words. Yet I could not resist a man with a soft voice and clean fingernails. They gave me such fine compliments: how my eyes are the colour of violets; my skin so fair and delicate; how charming my smile; and they quote poetry to add to the feeling. I jump at fine words like a child at candy. Each time I think, this time it will be different, but every man is your father all over again, in a fresh disguise. Talk. Talk. How could they talk. If it wasn't anarchism, it was socialism; if it wasn't atheism, it was religious fanaticism; if it wasn't Moses, it was Marx. Sometimes I wanted to talk, too. Things weren't that easy for me, and I wanted to tell someone about my troubles. They listened for a minute and got a funny look on the face like I remember from the idiot in my village. Once I said to Isaac —That awful Mrs. Silberman. Three bottles of dye I had to use on her hair, it's so thick and long. Naturally, I charged her extra. You should have heard her scream blue murder over the fifty cents. —Where you live up the hill, I told her, they would charge you double. I don't make profit on the dye. I called her a cheapskate. Anyway, it was her husband's money not her own she was fighting over. She called me a low-class low-life. I told her never to come back. Isaac didn't say I did right to throw her out. He explained to me about the capitalist class, and I said, —Don't give me the manifesto. You didn't see her ugly expression, I told him. And he said —Her actions were governed by the class struggle: she is the exploiter and you are the exploited. It was nothing against you personally, Lily. —But I'm the one she tried to cheat; I'm the one she cursed, may she rot in hell. —That's an ignorant approach to a classical social problem, Isaac explained —now, Lily, try and understand . . . Still, Isaac and me got along the best. He had consideration. He used to read to me while I was cooking late at night for the next day. On Sundays, we did the laundry together. He couldn't find a job, so he helped me what he could. I found little things for him to do, so he wouldn't feel useless. In the winter he carried out the ashes from the furnace from the store. He fixed the chairs and painted behind the shampoo sink. He was very artistic, the way he fixed up the windows with pictures and coloured paper. He made all my signs, like the "Specials" for the permanents. I was satisfied. Good or bad, nothing lasts forever.

Isaac decided to go into business for himself. Nobody can say I stopped him. I gave him the money to buy a stock of dry-goods to peddle on credit. He knew a lot of languages, but that didn't put money in his pocket. He spoke Russian, the customers cried in Russian; he talked in Ukrainian, they wept in Ukrainian; he sold towels in Yiddish, they dried their eyes on his towels. They prayed for help on his carpets; they lay sick between his sheets. How could he take their last cent, he asked me. So he gave everything away. Then he wanted more money for new stock. —I'm not the welfare department, I told him. The way he let people make a sucker out of him, I lost my respect. Then why did I marry him? God knows I didn't want to get married again: twice was enough. The government ordered me to get married.

Oh don't look so innocent. You think I don't know how all that court business started? It was you. You, with your long face and wet eyes, whining at other people's doors, like a dog, as if I didn't feed you right. I can imagine —Come in, come, Esther, sit down and have a piece of cake and tell me all about that terrible mother of yours. Women! Slaves, that's what they are, every one of them; yet if another woman tries to live her own life, they scream blue murder. I can see them, spending their empty nights talking about me, how I live with a man, not married. The Children's Aid wouldn't tell who snitched on me. Miss Graham, the social worker, was very nice, but she wouldn't say either. —I don't like to do this, she said, having to investigate reports from neighbours. Your daughter is thirteen years old and is paying a price in the community because her mother lives in sin. I said, —I am a decent, hard-working woman. See, my rooms are clean, look, my ice-box is full with fruit and milk, Esther is dressed clean, she never misses a day of school. A marriage license does not make a better wife or mother. She agreed with me, but there was nothing she could do. I had to marry Isaac or they would take away my daughter. I said, —This is a free country, I'll do what I want. So they summons'ed me to Family Court. —Your daughter, the judge said, needs a proper home. I told him, —Judge, Esther has a good home. She has a piano in her room and I pay for lessons. You should hear how nice she plays. —That is not the issue: it is a question of morality. —Judge, I said, I know all about morals and marriage. And what I don't know, the customers tell me. You should hear the stories. Is it moral, I asked him, for a woman to have to sleep with a man she hates? Is it moral for a man to have to support a woman whose face he can't look at? —Come, come, he said, these are not questions for this court to answer. We are here to administer the law. If you do not marry the man you are living with, we will take the child and place her with a decent family. Go fight city hall. So we took out the license and got married. I have bad luck. Isaac decided to write a book on the trade union movement in the textile industry. He stopped peddling: he stopped helping me. He talked of nothing but the masses: ate and slept the masses. So I sent him to the masses: let them look after him. Just shows how much the law knows what's best.

Love? Of course I loved him. For what other reason would I bother with a man if I didn't love him! I have bad luck, that's all. I attract weak men. Each time I think, aha, this one is different. It always begins with the compliments; it always ends with the silence. After he has been made comfortable in my bed, his underwear in my drawer, his favourite food in the ice-box, he settles down. I rush home from the store, thinking he is waiting for me. But no. He doesn't look up from the paper. He sits. I ask, —Do you want fish or herring for an appetizer? He says to the paper, —It doesn't matter. We eat. He sits. All I ask is a little consideration for all I do for them. Maybe once a week I would like to have a change. I wouldn't mind to pay for a show. I'm not ashamed to go up to the cashier and buy two tickets. Most women would make a fuss about that, but not me— I'm a good sport. I'm not one of your bourgeois women. That was your father's favourite word. Bourgeois. He said the bourgeois woman sold her soul for *kinder, kuchen* and *kirche*. See, I even remember a little German. That means— oh, excuse me! You know what the words mean—I forgot you are the clever one . . .

Hand me the towel. No, the one I use for the feet, the torn one. You're like a stranger around here, having to be told everything. I'll make a cup of tea. You can stay up a little later tonight: I feel like talking. No, sit. I'll make the tea, then you won't get in my way. What do you want with the tea—a piece of honey cake, maybe?

You and your father will get along, you're both so clever, Words, he had words for everything. No matter what the trouble was, he talked his way out of it. If there was no money for meat, he became a vegetarian, talking all the time how healthy fruits and nuts are; if he couldn't pay the rent, he spent hours complimenting the landlady on her beauty and charm, although she was fat and hairy; if I thought I was pregnant again, he talked about the joys of motherhood. When I cried day and night what would become of us, he talked the hospital into doing an abortion. But mouth work brings no food to the table. How was I to know that, young and inexperienced as I was? When I got married, I wasn't much older than you are now. I was barely seventeen when your father came home to Radom on a visit from the university in Zürich. It was before the war, in 1911. I was only a child when he fell in love with me. Yet, it can hardly be said I was ever a child: I was put to work at nine, gluing paper bags. At fourteen, I was apprenticed to a wig-maker. Every day, as I bent over the wooden form of a head, my boss would stand and stroke my hair, saying when I marry and have my hair shorn, he would give me a *sheitel* for a wedding present if I promise to sell him my hair for the wigs. My hair was beautiful, thick and silky, and a lovely auburn shade. I lasted three months, because his wife got jealous and dragged me back to my father by my silky hair. My father decided I must have done something wrong and beat me with his leather belt. What was there for me to look forward to, except more work, more misery, and, if I was lucky, marriage to a butcher's son, with red hands?

So you can imagine when your father began to court me, how could I resist? He had such fine manners, such an educated way of saying things, such soft hands, he was a man different from anyone I had ever met. He recited poetry by Goethe and Rilke, which he translated for me. He called me "*Blume*," which means flower, from a poem that starts, "*Du bist wie eine Blume*." He didn't want a dowry: I wouldn't have to cut my hair. He was a modern man: his views caused a scandal. Your father wasn't much to look at—short and pale and poor teeth. You know that small plaster statue of Beethoven on my dresser? The one you hate to dust? That belonged to him. He imagined he looked like Beethoven—he had the same high, broad forehead and that angry look. Still, to me his pale, shaven face was very attractive compared to the bearded men of the town. So we were married by a rabbi and I went back with him to Switzerland. Four years later, just before you were born, we were married in the city hall in Zürich so you would be legal on the records.

Let me see, how old is he now? I'm 38, so he must be 48. The *landsleit* say he never married again. I bet he never thought he'd ever see his daughter again. He won't be able to deny you: you're the spitting image. Pale like him. Same forehead, and the same red spots across when you get nervous. I'd give anything to be there when you're both reading and pulling at your hair behind the right ear. You certainly are your father's daughter. Even the way you sneaked around, not telling me, writing to Poland, until you got his address in Munich. I should have known you were up to something: you had the same look of a thief as him when he went to his meetings.

Those meetings! An anarchist he was yet. The meetings were in our small room. Every other word was "Revolution." Not just the Russian revolution, but art revolution, religious revolution, sex revolution. They were nearly all young men and women from the university, students like your father. Since he was a good deal older than the rest, he was the leader. They yelled a lot. At first I was frightened by the arguments, until I realized that these intellectuals didn't have anything to do with the things they fought about. It wasn't real people they knew, just names; it wasn't what they themselves did that caused so much disagreement—it was what other people somewhere else were doing. Where I come from, I was used to real trouble, like sickness and starvation and the threat of pogroms. So I didn't pay too much attention until the night we all had a big argument about Nora. First I should tell you about the young women who came to these meetings. They thought themselves the equal of the men, and the men treated them like comrades. Not like in Poland, where every morning of their lives, men thank God for not having been born a woman. In Zürich, the young ladies wore dark mannish suits, had their hair shingled and smoked cigarettes. Beside them, I felt like a sack of potatoes.

This play, *A Doll's House*, shocked everybody. Before you were born, your father sometimes took me to a play. For that, he found money. He called the theatre food for the soul. All such money-wasters he called his spiritual nourishment. I went anyway, because it was nice to sit in a big warm theatre, in a soft seat, and watch the actors. Remind your father about the night we saw *A Doll's House*. About ten of us came back to our room and talked until three in the morning about Nora. For the first time, I was able to join in. I was the only one who sympathized with the husband—he gave her everything, treated her like a little doll, loved her like a pet. This is bad? So they have a little argument, so she says she must leave him and the children. Leave the children! Did you ever hear such a thing! —The servants know how to run the house better than I do, she tells her husband. —Servants! I said to myself, there's your answer—she had it too good. If she had to struggle like me for a piece of bread, she would have overlooked her husband's little fit. She should have cooked him a nice supper, given him a few compliments and it would have all been *schmired* over, made smooth. Of course, I don't feel like that now, but that's what I thought the night I saw the play. The men agreed with me: it was stupid to leave a good life, even a bourgeois life, to slave for someone else as a seamstress. The women were disappointed in their comrades: couldn't these revolutionaries see that Nora was being exploited by her husband . . . ? The men argued that she was responsible for bringing up her children and should not have left them to the mercy of servants: that motherhood was sacred in all societies. The women said Nora was an intelligent, sensitive human being and was right to refuse to be treated like a possession, like a piece of furniture. Nora had to leave to keep her dignity and her pride. Exactly, the men said, dignity and pride are bourgeois luxuries. In the new society. . . . Back and forth the rest of the night.

All the next day, I could think of nothing but what Nora did. It never occurred to me that a woman leaves a man except if he beats her. From that time on, I began to change. I shingled my hair, I started to sit in the cafés and smoke. When I got pregnant again, I refused to go for an abortion. Four in three years was enough. I don't know why your father, with all his education, didn't know how to take care I shouldn't get in the family way. So you were born. Your father had to leave university and be a clerk in a shoe store. He hated the job: he hated me. You cried a lot. Nothing in your father's books explained why you cried so much. Then your father talked me into going back to work. They were glad to have me back at the beauty parlor. I was a good marceller. It was better to work than be stuck in a little room all day.

And the anarchist meetings started again. While everybody was making plans to blow up the world, I was busy running down the hall to the toilet to vomit. I was pregnant. —Well, look who's back they said at the clinic, —sign here, Lily. —I hope you will have it easier than me. Your father should send you to college. Maybe being educated will help, although sometimes I wonder. I met educated women who never knew what to do with themselves. Once, I remember, I asked one of my customers, *Frau* Milner was her name, —And how was the march yesterday for getting the vote for women? —It was called off, I couldn't lead the march to the city hall, she said, I got my period, only it was a miscarriage and I was hemorrhaging and couldn't get out of bed. —So you think the world is going to stand still until we stop bleeding?

What finally happened? What do you mean, finally? Things don't happen all at once. You want a drama like in a play, a big fight, with one person wrong, one person right . . . ? Nothing like that. I came back from the warm, clean hospital, where they were so kind to me, they looked after me like a child, I came back to a cold room, and dirty sheets, and our six dishes and two pots sticky with food.

Helen Weinzweig

There wasn't a penny for the gas and I couldn't heat your milk. You cried, your father yelled he couldn't study. After going to university for four years, I couldn't understand why he still needed to study. I had to get up six in the morning to take you to the crèche at one end of the city and go to work at the other end. You wouldn't stop screaming, and I spanked you, and your father said I was stupid to take out my bad feelings on an innocent child. I sat down, beaten. In that moment I knew I was going to leave. There is a second, no longer than the blink of an eye, when husband and wife turn into strangers. They could pass in the street and not know each other. That's what happened that night.

How did we get here? A good question, but a long story. We've talked enough; I'm tired. What's the difference now. Well, all right. You can tell your father how I did it: I want him to know I was not so stupid. He never knew I was getting a divorce until it was all over and I was out of the country. One of my customers was a very beautiful girl. She had long hair which I used to dye a beautiful shade of red, then I marcelled it in deep lovely waves from top to bottom. She came every Monday morning, and every week she would show me new presents from her lover. She was the mistress of a famous judge in Zürich. Her secret was safe with me: our worlds were miles apart.

One day, instead of going to work, I took you and went to the Court House. You were four years old; the war was over. I wasn't sleeping with your father because I was afraid of getting pregnant; and he wasn't sleeping at home much. At the Court House I bothered a lot of people where is Judge Sutermeister; I found out where he was judging. You were very good that morning while we sat outside on a bench, waiting. People smiled at us and asked you your name, and found things in their purses or briefcases to give you—pencils, paper, bon-bons, a small mirror. About twelve o'clock, when the doors opened and people came out, I stood in the doorway and watched where the judge went. He left through a door at the back. I went in with you, through the same door. He was sitting at a big desk, writing. Oh, he was an elegant gentleman, with gray hair. He looked very stern at me, and I almost ran away. I didn't wait for him to speak. I stood by his desk and told him my troubles, right away I said I wanted him to get me a divorce, and that I knew all about him and *Fräulein* Olga. He got up, he was so tall, and made such a big scene, like he was on stage; he was going to have me arrested. But I stood there, holding on to you and the desk. —And what will become of her if I go to jail? And what will happen to your career and your sweetheart if your wife finds out her money buys rings and pearls for your mistress? For the next six months, I kept on like usual. *Fräulein* Olga was the messenger for me and the judge. She didn't mind. She said it gave her something to do, asking me lawyer's questions, writing down my answers, bringing me papers to sign. One Monday morning, *Fräulein* Olga came with a large brown envelope holding my divorce papers. Inside also was a train ticket and some money. The judge wanted me to start a new life in America. I agreed. I remembered I had a cousin in Toronto. *Fräulein* Olga was very sad. —Who will do my hair? And she cried.

Two days later, I left our room with you. This time, we went straight to the train in Hamburg. We stayed near the station overnight. I bought underwear for us, a new sweater for me and a nice little red coat for you. We took the boat for New York. A sailor gave you a navy blue sailor hat with the name of the boat, *George Washington*, in gold on a ribbon around the hat. You wore it day and night, on Ellis Island, on the train to Toronto. It looked nice with the blond curls. I could go on and on. The things that happened, what I went through ... It's one o'clock already! Let's go to bed.

Helen Weinzweig

First, wash the cups. Wash them, I said. I can't stand a mess in the kitchen. Remember, never leave dirty dishes around. Show your father I brought you up right. Which reminds me: did you buy rolls like I told you? Good. Sam likes a fresh roll with lox for Sunday. Just think, in a week you will be on the ocean . . . Go already. I'll turn out the light . . .

QUADRILLE

Weekends at the cottage were not what they used to be. In the old days, two drinks were enough to create a guilty gaiety. Now, Jane and Walter Carruthers drank steadily without as much as a smile the entire weekend: she to chastise a wanton energy; he, as he boasted, to tie one on. No surprises were possible: they were alone most of the time and knew exactly what to expect of each other. Their friends, also middle-aged, were too busy to drive out to the Lake. The men had little empires to rule; their wives were either sick or attending the sick.

The three Carruthers children, almost grown, refused to stay grounded on the empty space between their parents. On Fridays, Jane drove out alone in her car. On Saturday afternoon, Walter in his.

On this particular Friday, the start of the long Queen's birthday holiday in May, young Ruthie Holmes had driven out with Mrs. Carruthers. After dinner they talked.

"Is your friend coming tonight or not?" Jane asked.

Jane was tired and would have liked to go to bed, but felt it her duty to wait up.

"He didn't know."

"Why not?"

"He's an artist, that's why not. He's not on schedule like a bus driver."

Ruthie went on to explain that Tom Harwood, her latest love, is unpredictable because he is a genius. Although he is the idol of the concert stage, Ruthie continued, he is, underneath, a shy, lonely man. She, Ruth, knows what is best for him, things like fresh air and true love. She asks only for the chance to prove her love. Jane was astounded that after so many disastrous liaisons, the girl was still taking a virginal posture. Ruthie had not changed very much in the twelve years she had known her, Jane reflected. The girl had been brought into the Carruthers household by their minister. She was sixteen and pregnant and frightened. They took care of Ruthie, saw her through the ordeal. The only thing the young woman learned from the experience, apparently, was not to become pregnant again. She continued to have fatal love affairs, the remains of which she always brought to Walter and Jane for decent burial.

At eleven, Ruthie washed off her make-up, a sure sign she was giving up hope.

"Maybe he will come tomorrow," Jane suggested.

"No. Tomorrow's Saturday. When he's not on tour, Tom goes to the chiropractor every Saturday morning, then rests all day."

"Ha! Some lover. Won't give up a backrub for you. I don't care if he is the reincarnation of Franz Liszt, he is still only a man. Haven't you got any pride?"

"Nope. I've tried pride and I stay home nights watching television. I guess he just can't bear to leave his Steinway."

"Formidable competition. How do you get yourself into these predicaments? Can't you find a man who isn't tied to someone or something?"

"You don't understand, you're married."

"Nonsense. Any girl can get married if she's determined to, especially an attractive girl like you. Not that I think marriage is so great, but what else is there? I don't believe in affairs. What did you get except heartaches from Bill, who couldn't risk the scandal of a divorce. And Charles couldn't bear to hurt his family. You really got taken by

John Williamson. For two years, you cooked his food and darned his socks, in return for which he anatomized you on page 87 of his book. They all love you in their fashion; then it's adieu, 'I would not love thee, dear, so much, loved I not honours, or money, or my picture in the paper, more.'"

"I can't help who I fall in love with," Ruthie was crying. "I am what I am. I go all out for a guy, I can't hold anything back. I can't play games like their wives do."

Jane was silent. What can you say to a young sophisticate who keeps falling for a line as old as sex?

Ruthie went on: "For instance, on Tom's birthday last month, I invited him to my apartment for dinner. It was to be a real celebration, just the two of us. I wore black chiffon harem pants. I bought oysters and champagne. He didn't show. At 9:30 I called his studio and said, well, hello, and he said, who's this? I discovered I had been defeated by a tricky passage in a Prokofieff sonata. But I didn't nag or scold. You see, I understand him."

"If a man doesn't have enough respect for me to remember a date I'd give him the gate. It shows a lack of respect. Whatever you may say about my marriage, there has always been respect. Walter respects me and I respect him."

"O.K., O.K., I get the point. So nobody respects me."

"That is not what I said. I said there must be respect between a man and a woman."

"Sure, that and a gallon of gas will get you to Convocation Hall for a free lecture on Saturday night. No thanks." Suddenly, Ruth moaned. "Oh, my head!" Her mouth was tight; she squinted with pain. "I'm getting one of my migraines."

"I'll get you some 222's."

"No, they won't help, pills don't work. I have to do something. Don't worry, I know how to lick this thing. I have to figure out my next move with that man, then I'll be all right."

"I don't know what you intend to do, but I've got to get some sleep so I won't be tired when Walter comes tomorrow. We get into some dandy snits if my nerves are bad."

"Oh. Forgot to tell you. Your husband is not coming out this weekend."

The older woman blinked at the stubs of candles sputtering on the dinner table. Slowly, she closed her thumb and forefinger over one feeble flame and then the other.

"Didn't feel a thing," she said, "maybe I have leprosy. How come you know my husband isn't coming? He said nothing to me."

Ruthie held her head to one side, as if something were aimed at her.

"Don't, Jane, not you too? I couldn't stand it if you turned against me. Suspicious men and jealous women— that's all I ever know. You and Walter are my best friends; yours is the only home I've ever had. I'd rather die than have you distrust me."

"I believe you. Just the same, you did stun me for a minute. Why did he tell you instead of me? That husband of mine has maintained a schedule you could set the town clock by: Walter Carruthers arrives at Hangover Haven every Saturday afternoon 3:25 on the button."

"Last Tuesday night, when I was at your place for dinner, Walter and I were chatting in the library. You had left for your Junior League meeting. Walter was pouring brandy like it was Pepsi, and I said how are things at the office and he said it's not his work, that's fine, but had you said anything to me about what's bothering you, you seem to be angry with him all time. Don't jump at me! I didn't bring up the subject—he did."

"Bothering me!" Jane's voice rasped with rage. He had no right to reveal to a stranger something they would not admit to each other. They had established the rules firmly in a secret code: keep up public appearances. Only behind the bedroom door were they free to avoid one another. "And what did you tell him?"

"I said you two are my best friends and I will not take sides. I refuse to get involved."

Now that's a neat scene, Jane decided: to be young and pretty and have everybody worry about you; to have your friends rush to your side in every skirmish; but when the winds of battle blow elsewhere, you wrap yourself snugly in a flag of neutrality and stay out of range of fire.

*

Quite early the next morning, the two women drove fifteen miles into Pinehurst, to the first large gas station. Ruthie headed for the 'phone booth next to the Coke dispenser. Jane got gas and had the car checked—yes, up for the weekend, hope so too, Joe, looks good so far, how's the family, we're all fine, thanks, Joe—Jane backed the car up against the whitewashed fence and waited. She could see Ruthie in the booth, her small round backside in pink stretch pants pushed against the glass door. Ruth dug into a large bag hanging from one shoulder and brought out a little black book. This she held up with one hand, secured the receiver against her ear between shoulder and head, and dialed with the other hand. She stood tense and unmoving. Then, in a sudden move, she dropped the little black book into the bag and wiggled a kind of bee dance. Outside the booth, as if on signal, the deserted gas station took on life. First came Joe, who leaned against a pump and slowly stroked its smooth sides as he watched Ruth. Then, Bert Ferguson followed and got a Coke from the machine, never once taking his eyes off the girl in the booth. Two more green-overalled young men emerged from the interior of the garage, wiping greasy hands on greasy rags. They all stood as if paralyzed, staring at Ruth. Any minute now, thought Jane, the four of them will move in unison, converge on their object, pull at the door, yank the girl out by her long, black hair and have at her, realizing fantasies nurtured in dark grease-pits. Jane had once asked her husband what exactly it was that made men go after Ruthie. He said, oh, I wouldn't. Jane said, I know, dear, I mean, other men. Well, he replied slowly, she has this expression on her face that says, try me, you may be surprised. I can't see it, Jane said. Of course not, Walter replied, she's like a daughter to you; you don't expect her to project all that—that—whatever it is—Sex, said Jane—all that stuff, Walter continued, when she's with the two of us.

Ruth bounced out of the booth, swinging her purse. Her triumphant grin embraced everyone. The men shifted self-consciously as if caught in the imagined act. They lowered their eyes and dropped their arms and took a few steps backward, then turned quickly to disappear into their Esso burrows. The girl got into the car, slammed the door, and did a cha-cha on the floorboard.

"Come on, let's go. Little Ruthie knows more than one way to skin Tom cats. I talked to Sidney. He promised to drive him out this afternoon. Tom will go anywhere with Sidney. He's always worried about an accident to his hands, but feels safe if Sidney drives."

"Who's Sidney?"

"Sidney Standish, as in Standish Steel. I think Sidney would like to forget his money started with Poppa Steinberg and a wagon full of scrap metal. Sidney paid for Tom's lessons for years, as well as sponsoring his Carnegie Hall recital. Naturally, Tom is devoted to his patron. I don't much care for the gentleman, he's always on the defensive, and very cynical, but I have to play up to him if I want Tom. The first time Tom came to see me, he brought Sidney. That was some ordeal. Here I'm trying to make an impression and Sidney just sits there, silent, just looks as if he'd like to split. He made me feel that everything I wore, the way I looked, the things I said—they were all wrong. But love me, love my Sidney. So I learned to take it from the guy, not that you can fool him for a second but he admired my persistence, I think. He was almost pleasant when I 'phoned just now. He'll drive Tom out as soon as he can."

They were on the narrow back road. Jane stopped the car.

"Do you realize the spot you've put me in? I don't mind pretending to chaperon you and Tom, but what in the world do I do with Sidney? You'll have to 'phone back and call it off. No, better not. He'll think it's an anti-Semitic plot." She started the car, driving slowly. "Guided tour anyone? To your right and to your left and as far as the horizon, are members of the Establishment, related to one another by blood, the kind that is drawn quarterly. And as we arrive at the Carruthers compound, we find the guest house, reserved for my in-laws, whose whimsical habit it is to drive out from Toronto to surprise the children. It's going to be extremely awkward to explain the two strange men staying with us."

"They'll only be here for the day. It never occurred to me you'd object to my friends. You always encouraged me to bring them to your house."

"In the city, yes, but not to this goldfish bowl." They had arrived at the cottage. Jane shut off the motor and sat at the wheel, thinking. Ruth was quiet, in that still way of hers, like a cat in tall grass, waiting for something to move. "It isn't me, it isn't me," Jane protested, "it's my position. I married a whole tradition. Oh, Lord. Jews and beatniks. I can't put out a sign saying they're your friends, not mine. By the way, what will you tell Walter?"

"I don't have to tell him anything," Ruth said, "he's your husband."

"Thank you."

Jane got out of the car and slammed the door. She went down to the lake and walked all the way to the Perkins dock and back, twice.

*

The men arrived about one. Under the tall, old pines, Tom Harwood was not the impressive stage figure: he was slight and boyish. He wore a dirty beige corduroy jacket over an undershirt; stained cotton trousers, with a safety pin fastened over a zipper which had obviously failed. "The sonofabitch didn't give me time to dress. Boy," he held his pale face up to the sun, "doesn't that feel good. Listen to those goddamn birds imitating Puccini." Sidney, beside him, looked around as if in a foreign country. Jane extended a sporting hand towards him. She was relieved to see that he looked no different than her husband's business associates—tall and fair and carefully dressed in grey worsted. As she pumped his hand, he read her face and she knew at once he had found her out. She became too effusive, too happy they were able to come, too eager they come right in and have a drink. Sidney said nothing, looked nothing, didn't help her out with a single pleasantry, made no attempt to lighten her guilt. Tom handed her the paper bag he had been cradling, the contents of which were easily divined: only the Liquor Control Board issued brown paper bags that size and shape.

Indoors, Tom discovered the old Bell piano, a huge rococo instrument, to which he attached himself like a child to a toy. He played Scarlatti and drank gin with equal intensity. Off in a corner on a rocker, Sidney listened and watched, declined a drink. Ruthie was restless. "Oh come on, Tommy," she said, "let's dance." She made him stand up, then opened the lid of the piano bench and pulled out a pile of old sheet music. While Sidney looked on, remote as a stranger in a crowd, the others went ahead with the

business of having a good time. They sang and drank and
pranced about; they mimed the archaic pictures on the
covers of the old popular ballads. "Dad, Oh Dad, You Have
Been More Than a Father to Me, You Have Been a Mother."
Ruthie clung to Tom and sang, "Hold Me, Hold Me, Parson,
I'm Getting Religion." With each song and with each refill,
the noise increased. Sidney would not be persuaded to join
in. Jane felt sorry for him, the way he sat and rocked, not
having any fun at all. She floated over to his corner as if
on ball-bearings and hung over him, heavy-breasted,
steadying herself on the arm of his chair.

"You people," she said, "don't know how to enjoy your-
selves. All you care about is—" She couldn't remember.

Abruptly he stood up, side-stepping her demanding
presence.

"It's stuffy in here," he said, and flung open a window.

"Shut that window!" Jane shouted, "you want the neighbours to hear us?"

She was at the window, pushing down on it with one
hand balancing a full glass with the other; and as she
banged the window shut, the liquor spilled down the front
of her dress. For the first time his expression changed; he
had the satisfied look of a man whose adversary had
slipped in the mud. He took out a handkerchief and wiped
the stains.

"You people," he said, "drink too much."

As he mopped at her, Jane began to giggle like a girl.
She sang with the music, "How Come You Do Me Like You
Do-do-do," and smiled at him in boozy intimacy. Unexpectedly, he laughed a deep, clear laugh that managed by
surprise to disinfect their high spirits. A sterile silence followed. Tom's back rounded over the keys; he began to play
quietly. Chopin. Ruthie said, "This isn't Massey Hall, no
concerts please." She pulled Tom to the door. Jane and Sidney were still facing one another at the window. She stood,

uncertain whether to stay or go, feeling left behind, stranded, isolated in her own home.

"What would you like to do?" she asked Sidney.

"It doesn't matter."

"Would you like to take a walk?"

"Would you?"

"Oh no! I can't! I mean, I have things to do."

"Then I'll keep you company."

"Oh no! I mean, I'll be busy."

He refused to be dismissed. He looked beyond her at the wall, at summer pictures neatly hung, of three generations of Carruthers. He yawned.

"I'm sorry you're bored," Jane said, more in anger than in sorrow. "Why did you come if you intended to be bored?"

"Boredom is my only refuge; it is the human condition I'm most familiar with. Frankly, I'm not sure why I came. I change one kind of monotony for another, I suppose. Also, Tom has been working hard and I thought I'd bring him out for a bit of diversion: you know, make out with his broad."

"You're nothing but a pimp!" The word didn't sound so dreadful; she was almost proud of having thought of it. And the accusation must move him to do something. Surely. He only looked at her with some wonder, as if she had just now materialized.

"Careful. The enamel is chipping. You know damned well what your little Ruthie is up to. She's on the make for Tom and by any other name you're procuring too. Insulting me doesn't absolve you. Where, dear madam, are your manners? Remember, I was invited, I am your guest!"

"You people invoke the rules to your advantage: you play the game only when it suits you. I know all about your morality—screw the *shiksas* but keep our Jewish girls pure."

"I see you subscribe to all the myths. What else do you

believe—that we commit ritual murder; that we own Eaton's and Simpson's?"

A great discomfort assailed her. She was on alien ground. He had come into her castle and lured her out into his camp. How does one deal with a man who refuses casual contact and who insists upon entering into the heart of the matter?

"I'm sorry I was rude," she tried.

He moved away from the window, letting go of her, as it were. He said, "Forget it. Any sort of honesty is better than false small-talk."

"I appreciate your frankness. But don't get too honest with me: I'm not used to it."

"It's a deal. Let's get out. They tell me you have beautiful country out here."

It's a free country, Jane thought, yours as well as mine. But she was afraid of further misunderstanding, and kept silent.

They walked on a hot road, away from town, deeper into the countryside. Week-enders were out in the hot spring sun. Jane waved to them, her old friends and neighbours, but they did not wave back. About a mile down the road they stopped while Sidney removed pebbles from his shoes. He had begun to limp: the coarse gravel would be hard under the thin soles of his shoes. Jane said, "Over here, it's softer on the grass." And they walked single-file, he in front, on the narrow strip of soft earth beside the ditch. The ineffable peace lasted about two minutes. An open sports car came roaring towards them. It careened madly from side to side on the road, as if no one was at the wheel. Jane's first reaction was to see whose car it was. There was no time. Sidney threw himself into the shallow ditch and pulled her down after him, one arm around her waist to keep her from falling, his other hand spread across her face.

"Don't look," he said.

Of course she had to find out what it was she shouldn't
look at. As the car swerved towards them, tilted, straightened out again, she saw three young men, as souped up
as their motor. One of them was totally naked. He sat on
the rim of the far door, his delicate pale rump over the edge.
He was clutching his genitals. His face, as white and bare
as the rest of him, was twisted in a blind paroxysm of union
with himself.

"On our road!" Jane exclaimed, in an attempt to disguise
her fascination at the sight, "imagine a thing like that on
our road."

"Our road!" Sidney mimicked, "there you go again. This
sort of thing simply must not happen on our road. Is that
all you feel—no concern, no pity, for those poor kids?"

"I can't imagine who they are," she continued to make
blundering sounds, to draw his attention from the nest of
the truth: that the boy's passion was contagious, that she
was fighting off the need to similarly take hold of a spread-
ing ache.

"No one you know, I'm sure."

She was safe; he was disgusted with her.

Sidney clambered awkwardly out of the ditch, then
pulled her up. He stood against the bright sky, his head
high, at an angle, listening. Only a soundless hum surrounded them. She stood at a slight distance, like a
respectful novitiate waiting to be summoned for instruc-
tion. Sidney ignored her. He darted forward and ran,
half-limping, as if on a road-bed of nails. She loped easily
behind. At one point, he tossed his jacket back at her—"look
after this," he ordered. After about sixty yards he halted,
red-faced and out of breath. Then he started to shout,
"Tom!" over and over. What must have been on his mind
from the time they saw the drunken boys, slowly filtered
from his thoughts to hers, and she too began to fear. "Ruth!"
she alternated with his calls. The road ended at an aban-

doned sawmill. Jane knew the place well. It had been a playground for the summer children, who spent rainy days in games in the decrepit mill and blacksmith shop. Jane recalled the last time, about five years ago, Ruthie had followed the children into the dark mill. When she came out, her computer eyes were programmed with future plans.

By now Jane was well ahead of Sidney, into the lumber yard.

"Stop! Wait!" he shouted at her, "stay where you are."

She paid no attention: this was her bailiwick, she would go where she pleased, he had no right to tell her what to do. He caught up with her. He was sweating with determination.

"You do as I say. Wait right here. This is a man's job."

Jane let her shoulders droop and hung her head in what she hoped was an air of submission. And what one pretends to feel, as sometimes happens, one begins to feel. And so Jane stood in the open yard, experiencing a strange helplessness. She waited for him as a rock waits for shadows to be cast upon it. He finally emerged from the mill. He put an arm around her shoulders and said with triumph, "The kids are safe." He led her towards the mill, and as she walked beside him, she was careful to keep her steps short.

They found Ruth sunning herself behind the blacksmith shop. Her face reflected nothing but light. Only her closed eyelids flickered for an instant as they stood over her. To Sidney's question she replied, "He's still in there, sitting on his hands." They went inside and waited for their eyes to adjust to the darkness. There wasn't a sound. Sidney addressed himself to the rafters in a paternal voice: "It's all right, Tom, I'm here; there's nothing to be afraid of. Come down."

"I can't get down," they heard. Jane followed the sound

and made out Tom's form crouched against the slant of the roof.

"Come down the way you went up," Sidney coaxed.

"I don't know how I got up here," Tom answered like a plaintive child.

Shades of the old loggers, Jane thought, they'd have pounded each other into hysteria at the sight of this dude clinging to an upright. Jane was about to climb up and rescue him—how often she had gone after a recalcitrant son—when she remembered her new role. She groped and tripped and chattered nonsense, until she came to the place against the east wall that the kids had used for climbing. Here was a solid beam into which large nails had been driven for foot-holds. Tom had only to crawl about three feet, slip through an opening between boards and slide down. But it was not Tom she was concerned with. It was this man, this Sidney, who was acting like some ancient tribal leader.

Sidney came over and once again handed her his jacket. He climbed half-way up the beam, talked Tom into leaving his sanctuary, and helped him down. When finally the three of them were outside, Sidney took inventory of his friend.

"O.K., boy?"

Tom held his hands up before his eyes, pulled at the fingers, one by one, as if counting them.

"I think so," he said.

Sidney addressed his little band, "Now then, you three, wait here. Stay clear of the road. Watch out for those boys, they may be back. I'll get my car." His face was grey, his step uneven. Jane felt sorry for him.

"Let me walk back with you," she suggested, "I'm not tired."

It was a mistake. He became irritated. She tried to joke, "I'm used to forced marches."

"But not used to taking orders, just giving them."

She wanted to retort, oh come off that persecution bit, but decided to let him have the last word. This was neither the time nor place to challenge him.

Tom slumped down beside Ruthie and looked into her eyes for sympathy. Ruth turned her back on him. Tom got up and circled around her feet and sat down in front of her again. He reached for her hand. Ruthie drew back, then jumped up and said, "I'm getting the hell out of here; I won't breathe the same air as this creep." Sidney grabbed her as she ran past. "Now then, you three, stay put and stay together until I come back."

They had to wait almost an hour. Ruthie burned with sun and rage. Tom sat on a broad tree-stump, his head almost down to his knees, drawing clefs and staves in the sawdust with a short stick. Jane was surprised at her own lack of interest in the other two. It was like minding someone else's children: it didn't matter really whether they behaved or not—they weren't hers to worry about. Jane made no effort to reconcile them. Everyone to his own corner, choose your own weapons, fight your own battles, she told herself. Time to look out for number one. Ruthie would form some other unsatisfactory attachment; Tom would go back to his music. And Sidney? Where is the focus of his life? He goes from what to what? She had to know, she would find a way.

*

They drove in silence back to the cottage. Sidney kept the motor running while the women, in the back seat, got out. Ruthie slammed doors, car and cottage. Tom slid close to his friend. Jane stood beside Sidney's open window, smiled and waited, from force of habit mostly, for the courtesies. Had a lovely time, do come back, thank you so much again, safe journey. Not a word. Sidney just stared ahead, and when she moved out of the way, revved up the motor and drove off.

Jane felt she had been defeated without a fair fight. She had endured his hostility; she had submitted to his domination. It had been a change from the usual stalemate of her marriage.

Ruthie was in the big bedroom, combing her long hair.

"What are you so happy about?" Ruth demanded, "the day was a total disaster." Whatever the nature of her struggles, there was always a decent finality about Ruthie's duels. "I've had it," she went on, "every man I've ever cared for has failed me, one way or another." She peered into the mirror: there were no visible scars. Jane stretched out on the bed and listened to her young friend with a new attentiveness, thinking maybe I can learn something from this child. "You should have seen Tom when those boys drove into the yard. He was scared to death. Who, me? I eat boys like that for breakfast. They were full of booze and only wanted to show off. That's all. They horsed around and teased us, friendly-like. I treated them like schoolkids playing hookey. They offered to leave us some beer. But Tom was shaking like a leaf and they kept staring at him. I don't think they'd ever seen anything like Tom before—a pale, skinny guy with long blond hair and long white hands. Then one guy noticed that safety pin on his pants. 'Look what's holding this cat together, I bet he falls apart if we take it off,' one of them said, and reached for the pin. Tom ran. The worst thing he could have done. 'Get that fag,' they yelled. They ran after him into the mill. I could hear them laughing and shouting in there. Then two of the boys came out, waving clothes around. I was relieved when I saw they weren't Tom's. Then this third boy comes running out of the mill, stark naked, chasing after his clothes. 'Here's a real man for you, lady,' somebody said. They came towards me. I was holding a long chunk of iron in both my hands. 'One more step,' I told them, 'and I'll ruin this punk for life.' They thought that was very funny, but they left me alone just the same. They turned around and started chasing the naked kid, who headed for their car. How do you figure it, Jane, shouldn't Tom have stayed to protect me? Aren't there any men left who will take care of a woman?"

"They say Jewish men are good to their wives."

"That isn't what their wives say; they complain same as you. You just don't know *men*."

"I'm willing to learn."

"Do you suppose those kids were right, that Tom is a homosexual?"

"You're the expert on men. You should be able to find out."

"I would if I could, but he never stays around long enough. And then there's always Sidney. What about that Sidney, huh? Do you suppose they're more than just buddy-buddies?"

"Not the way you mean, I'm sure. Sidney just wants to take care of people. You know—bring me your needy and helpless. He simply is too serious about it, that's all. Now if we can coax him into holding a martini in his outstretched hand, we might separate him from Tom."

Silence. Jane felt she'd tipped her hand. Ruth deliberated for a while, then decided she wanted no partner in her game. Ruthie said, "I don't care, it doesn't matter. I never want to see Tom again."

*

In the middle of the night Jane, who had not slept, got out of bed and went into the living room. Using a flashlight, she found Ruth's bag on the floor beside the couch. Quite deliberately she took out the little black book, looked under "S" and copied out Sidney's telephone number. She walked around the dark room for quite some time with the slip of paper between her fingers. Then she located her own purse and removed the wallet with its plastic windows revealing licence, and credit cards. She folded the slip of paper neatly, twice, and carefully hid it between the metal plates for Eaton's and Simpson's.

CAUSATION

The woman hesitated at first to let him in. "Piano tuner," Gyorgi Szigeti said, then waited, leaning against the door frame. He waited for her to decide whether he was a musician and therefore eligible to come in the front door, or whether he was a tradesman to be directed to the rear entrance. What she could not have known was that Gyorgi had no intention of using the servants' entrance. He stood before her, proud in his black bowler hat, his long white silk scarf knotted loosely and flowing down over his shiny black leather jacket. "Piano tuner," he repeated to the woman, who had not moved. She was transfixed. "Oh my God," she said, "not you, not you!" He did not question her words: by habit he took no notice of the eccentricities of the rich. Slowly, slowly, she widened the doorway.

No one ever had to show him where the piano was. He found it the way a dog searches out a bone. Traversing miles, it seemed, of Oriental carpets to reach the ebony grand piano at the other end of a vast room, he experienced a numbness, a detachment, as if asleep and dreaming: he had a sense of having once before covered the distance. And the short, sturdy woman in a flowered housecoat (he had noticed) who was following him—he knew her, too. But then, he knew a lot of women, some also short and sturdy, and maybe that's all it was: so many women.

"It's my own piano," she was saying. Her heavy hand clumped across the keys. "This B keeps getting out of tune," striking the note five times to let him hear how bad it was.

Gyorgi Szigeti almost fell to his knees. He was in the presence of a Bechstein grand piano.

She was still talking. "Everything you see in here, all the furniture in the house, was chosen by my ex-husband. He lets me keep my piano only because he is a music lover."

Gyorgi removed his black leather jacket, draping it on the back of a gilded chair with curved legs. The bowler hat and silk scarf he arranged carefully on the seat. He ran his fingers over the piano keys. The sound was as brilliant as he remembered a Bechstein to be; the base was resonant and the top notes vibrant. This was unexpected: in these wealthy homes the pianos were regarded as furniture and tuned only when an anticipated house guest was some sort of performer.

"I'm a singer. A concert artist. An opera star," she announced. "That is, I used to be an opera star."

While Gyorgi worked, she sat on the piano bench, which he had moved aside. She hummed each note in unison with his repeated plunking as he tightened strings. She had perfect pitch. It spurred him on, this breathless attention of hers; then the two of them listening, listening together, both now intent on the climactic moments when he brought each white whole note and each black half note to perfection. He felt like the Creator of All Sound. When he tightened a string, he had a way of tightening his mouth, twisting the left corner upward into his cheek, which resulted in a threatening grimace. Once the ideal sound was achieved, his mouth loosened.

She rose to leave. "Would you like some coffee?"

Gyorgi looks around, then re-enters the room in his mind, retraces his steps in imagination; but this time, instead of seeing her figure stride out the doorway, as it is doing at this very moment, he sees her laid out in a satin-lined coffin, in the same flowered housecoat; and instead of her sluttish make-up, the face in death is delicately tinted as if in the blush of youth. The mortician's skill has fixed the happiness he, Gyorgi, gave her. After the funeral he stays on in the old house, sleeping in one of the spare rooms, surprised at his delicacy, even in fantasy, in not using the bedroom where he had made her ecstatic. The letter from the lawyers comes, addressed to Gyorgi Szigeti, to this house. She has left him everything. Everything, including the beloved Bechstein, is his. Just in time, before her return interrupts his fateful vision, he recalls with a sudden clarity the source of his images: an account in this morning's newspaper: rich elderly widow . . . a young man of thirty-three . . . they married . . . she died . . . left him everything owned . . . great wealth . . . her daughters suing . . . old mother was crazy . . . *"They're crazy,"* the new heir had protested to the judge, "she was more fascinating, more of a woman, than those two dried-up broads will ever be if they live to be a hundred."

Over coffee, perhaps because he had already lived out the scene in his mind, Gyorgi leaned forward and said in a voice deep with sincerity:

"You are still a beautiful woman. You have so much to give . . ."

She eyed him silently. She was about fifty-five, but in her clear, light eyes, raised to meet his directly, age had been postponed. It was a matter of pride with him that in his persuasions Gyorgi rarely lied. In every woman he found qualities he could honestly admire. He went on, emboldened:

"Your eyes—they are the eyes of a girl."

She denied nothing: that was all that mattered.

"These Bechsteins," he ventured, "do not take kindly to the extreme cold and intense heat of our climate. The wood ...changes of temperature..." He brought out a small notebook from his back pocket. He could come back next week. To see if the tuning held.

*

Uppermost in her mind is the fact that his wide, curved mouth is at odds with his small, deep-set, dark eyes, suggesting to her an easygoing cruelty.

*

At his ring the following week she flung open the door. Her face was heavier than before with rouge and lipstick, her brows blacker, her lids greener. Gyorgi believed that if he ate enough of the stuff women put on their faces he would get cancer. In such cases he would put his lips to the bare hollows of her throat.

Today she ignored his pretence of tuning the perfectly tuned instrument. She didn't listen; she chattered.

"Once I was Violetta with the San Francisco Opera Company. Oswald, my former husband, loved *Traviata*. He loved me. He offered me the world if I would give up the stage and sing for him alone: wealth, babies, a fire in the hearth on Sunday nights. Oh, he knows his operas... I worked hard, practised every day. In the evening, with the two babies asleep in the nursery, I sang for him. I dressed for the part. The costumes accumulated: Cio-Cio San, Carmen, Tosca, Mignon.

"The idyll lasted almost five years. One morning I awoke to find him standing at the foot of the bed. The room was still dark so that I could not quite see his face, just the outline of his figure, fully dressed. He had been waiting, I sensed, for me to awaken. I sat up and then he spoke, slowly and distinctly:

" 'You are not the great artist I thought you were. You

cannot place your voice, and when it comes out from behind your big nose, the glorious music falls to the floor like a bag of cement. You are ridiculous in the clothes of the great heroines: you have the passion of a disposable lighter. You have deceived me.' With that, he left and never returned."

"Did he leave you for another woman?" Gyorgi asked, for that is what he knew of the way of the world.

"No, no, he wouldn't do that. He is a very respectable man."

"Did he marry again?"

"Ha! The only woman he'd consider would have to be a virgin who chose marriage to Oswald instead of entering a nunnery." She gave him a sly smile. "You know what? I think Oswald was jealous of my music. When I sang Mimi or Aïda or Desdemona, I became the woman I was portraying. I didn't mean to, but I escaped him each time—*that's* what he couldn't stand."

Gyorgi tilted his head in a pretense of interest. He had no idea what she was talking about, but he realized that she was determined to reveal herself to him. It was as if women had to expose themselves—their defeats, their triumphs, their hopes and beliefs—before they undressed. In his opinion, a nude man in a raincoat was more honest. Gyorgi listened to women for their "tone" quality, the same way he listened when he was tuning a piano. He noticed that her forehead glistened with perspiration.

"I can't pay you today," she said. "Oswald has gone to India to see his guru. Left me without a cent. Again."

"It's all right," he said gently, "you can pay any time."

*

Even after she had paid him, Gyorgi took to dropping in, making his visits sporadic, so that they would seem compulsive, as if he couldn't resist seeing her. She was always unprepared, and would run to comb her hair and put on fresh lipstick. Once he stopped her, saying he liked her the way she was. Above all, he would want her to be perfectly natural with him. She was so moved by these sentiments, she wanted to do something for him in return.

"Would you like to hear Cio-Cio San's farewell aria? No? I see. But you obviously know everything about pianos."

"I was an apprentice for five years in the Bechstein factory in Berlin."

"What else can you do?"

"I can build a bomb shelter."

"Good. Then you can take care of this house. What do you say—live here and look after things. Oh, you will go out to your work as you always have, but instead of a small room in a smelly boardinghouse—ah, I thought so!—you can stay here. Pick any of the five spare rooms. What do you say?"

Gyorgi couldn't speak. He put his hands on his lap lest she see how they shook. A mansion, a Bechstein—all within the space of a few weeks. He hung his head and assumed the obsequious manner of his youth.

Then he went through the house, taking the stairs two at a time. The rooms were full of the kind of masterpieces he had seen only behind thick silken cords in museums. Everything was old and massive or old and fragile; everything was forceful with value. She ran after him, unable to keep up, observing that he moved with an animal grace, as if he had lived all his life out of doors.

"I can't understand why a man would want to leave you. It's a wonderful house," he said.

"Oswald doesn't care about material things—furniture, cars, clothes—he has no interest in them. He wants to touch the infinite, discover the ineffable; he is on a journey of the spirit, he is concerned only with his immortal soul."

"So?" said Gyorgi. "So?" he repeated, "He has never had to work hard in order to eat."

"You must know that I still love him."

Suddenly she was crying, crying for no reason that he could see.

He waved an arm into the air, around and around. "You have everything; you have it all!"

"Nothing! Nothing, I tell you. There is only the music, notes on a page, enduring, eternal, nothing else exists." Then, in after-thought, her voice distant, she added, "You are the exception."

He chose the sixth bedroom. Hers. Awaiting her in the wide bed, he called out, "And wash that damned crap off your face."

When she came back into the room, she grasped the post at the foot of the huge bed, weaving slightly as if drunk, and intoned:

"I adore you, you are low-born, you have no character, you are inevitable. Ours will be an affair of terrible limits. Your insults are without principle. Whatever grief you will cause will come naturally and I shall recover as one does after slipping on ice. Most important, though, Oswald will no longer be able to draw blood with his blunt knives. I shall continue to go to him every week for money. But it will be for you. That will make it easy. No. More than that. I shall *enjoy* the humiliation. I will answer his interrogation: 'Why is the butcher's bill so high?' 'Because I have a tall, strong man to feed.' I will sit in the leather chair in his office while he counts out the ten–dollar bills, slowly, sliding them halfway across the desk. I will lean forward and scoop them up and thank him. Oswald will unbutton his vest and look across at me like a judge with a three-time loser and condemn me, as he always does, with good advice. But I won't care. He has lost his power: tonight I hand it over to you."

*

During the prolonged love-making that follows, she opens her eyes a few times. Once she sees his mouth tighten and a corner go up into his cheek into an ugly grimace.

*

Gyorgi moved in. It was then that he was faced with what he had missed that first time because his head had been burning with the delirium of his good fortune. There was everywhere a fury of disorder, as if a bomb had gone off in each room separately. The halls had boxes and over-shoes strewn about. There was dirt on every surface; old dust that had hardened; mouse droppings in the kitchen and cockroaches in the sinks. She shrugged off his dismay. "Oswald won't pay for a cleaning woman."

Gyorgi loved control and completeness. He set about to restore order, spending every weekend sweeping, scrubbing, repairing, room by room, starting with the bedroom. The kitchen alone took a month. The cellar, he figured, could occupy him as long as she lived.

There was no design to her life. Asleep when he left, off in a world of song when he got home, she could not remember what, if anything, she had accomplished, nor what had transpired during the day. "Some phone calls. Nothing much. How was *your* day?" And showered him with kisses. One of the phone calls, he surmised, was for the frozen chicken pie and canned pea soup that he was eating for dinner. And he, who required a daily pattern to blanket his years, felt a chill of apprehension.

"Now, my handsome Magyar," she crooned, "I'll sing for you and you alone. I learned some Hungarian folk songs set by Kodály."

"I told you a dozen times, I hate Hungarian anything. Maybe there's a soccer game on tv."

"Don't you ever tire of watching grown men kick a ball?"

"You have the memory of an imbecile: I told you: I was a professional soccer player. I toured Germany."

*

Each day Gyorgi went out on his calls. He had given up his black leather jacket and now wore a navy blue blazer with a crest embroidered in red and white on the upper left pocket. He refused to part with his bowler hat and long white scarf. He no longer said, "Piano tuner," at the front door. Instead, he presented, wordlessly, his business card with his name and elegant new address and *Pianos Tuned to Perfection* embossed in shiny black script. As the days got shorter, he came home earlier and earlier. Some cold days he did not go out at all. He would float about the house, content to hammer, force windows open, stop taps from dripping. She would follow him around like the small daughter he once had. While he worked, she would sit on the floor, always in the flowered housecoat, telling him stories about people she knew.

"You're making it up," he sometimes accused her. "No, no," she protested, "that's what he really did." Or, "She was desperate. A woman in that state will say anything." His disbelief at times bordered on wonder: did people of wealth and substance really carry on crazy like that? Keeping his eyes on his work, never turning his head, pretending a lofty indifference, he would probe with ruttish questions: what had taken place with her and Oswald in bed; what had she done with other men; how many lovers; in what combinations. And she, without a second thought, would lay open intimacies as one spreads open an umbrella in the rain. And always she hugged her knees and chortled deep in her throat, "But you, my darling, are the best, you are the champ." On those days a camaraderie was struck between them and he felt himself to be her equal in the sense that she was no better than he. More than that: he felt himself elevated, and ceased to regret, once and for all, that he was so unschooled that she had to read to him the instructions on a can of varnish.

*

Every night he made love to her. He treated the whole business as his part of the bargain. In bed his movements were as easy and as graceful as when he painted a wall or repaired a broken drainpipe. He was precise; he was unhurried. Afterwards, Gyorgi would turn over as if fatigued, although his exultation was boundless. He did this rather than listen to her. "You talk too much," he would say, "people screw up by talking too much."

Once she frightened him in the middle of the night by shaking him awake. The bedside lamp was on. She was sitting bolt upright.

"Quickly," she said in an urgent voice, "don't think, tell me, quickly, what is life?"

"Life," he said obediently, "is. Life is. That's all. You're either alive or dead."

"Wrong!" she said sharply. "Life is an imposition. Oswald refuses to admit it. He wants life to be raw, with the bones showing. Today he presented me with a new account book, with more spaces for more entries. He threatened me again, unless I am more exact about the money I spend, he will cut off my alimony. He *imposes* himself on my life."

Gyorgi condescended. "What are you complaining about? A short ride in the Mercedes and you're living fat for another week. Perfect octaves don't buy houses like this."

"You comprehend nothing." She turned from him. "You

know nothing of the malice that masquerades as virtue. You are young: you still make plans."

He stared at the long, heavy drapes.

"After the war we were thrown out of Hungary and shipped in boxcars to Germany. We lived behind barbed wire, then in barracks, then in a shack somewhere outside Frankfurt. All night long we heard the screams of the tortured. My brothers and sisters and I jumped out of bed when we heard the cries. We took turns standing on a chair at the small, high window. We could see nothing. Our parents never woke up."

She studied him: there was no humility in him. She laid her head on his chest and a hand on his shoulder. Gyorgi yawned and lay back with his hands under his head.

"Fate," she whispered, "weaves its mysteries in the dark; that is why we do not know our destiny in the light of day."

"That's true," he agreed, understanding nothing. He had no sense of the abstract, but he recognized, if not destiny, certainly an opportunity. "You have a beautiful house. I'm surprised you never married again."

"Oswald wouldn't like it. Besides, if I married I wouldn't have this beautiful house."

Gyorgi, startled, heard only the first part: "Oswald wouldn't like it." What did Oswald have to do with her desire to marry again? His own life had been a series of divorcements so immutable that he never again saw his parents, his brothers and sisters, two wives, countless lovers, as well as a number of unreasonable employers. If his decision to part, made simply and honestly, was challenged, he used his soccer-field fists, elbows, knees, or boots to make his meaning clear.

"We are lovers now," he pursued, "let us be as if married. I will care for you as my father did for my mother; you will care for me as my mother did my father."

"But you are already here, in my house, in my bed . . . "

Lack of sleep made Gyorgi irritable. She was missing the point.

"From now on," he rasped, "you will do a woman's work."

"Oh, oh," she moaned, "more impositions . . . "

"We must speak of necessities," he went on inexorably. "Food is a necessity. Respect is a necessity. It is necessary to respect the place you eat and sleep in. The way you live now, you turn roses into shit. Starting tomorrow, you will keep the house clean, wash the clothes, cook the meals. I will take out the garbage, attend the mousetraps, spray the roach powder."

"My music . . . "

"*Deine stimme is zum kotzen,*" he said as day dawned, "you have the voice of a crow."

"Yes, yes," she said, falling in with his thought, "I will buy a loom and learn to weave."

"Don't be stupid. You're too clumsy."

She flung her faith into the new day. Laughing now and clapping her hands she exclaimed:

"You noticed! Oh, how I do love you!"

*

She no longer rouges her lips and cheeks nor colours her eyelids. Gyorgi has convinced her of his preference for an unadorned face. This he has done by holding her head down in the bathroom sink filled with water. Her giggles spluttered, she choked, she lost consciousness. She has learned that he means what he says. She thinks he has helped her begin a new life. She telephones everyone she knows to tell them that she gets up in the morning and that she bakes bread.

CAUSATION

*

Just before Christmas there was a party. Gyorgi was surprised, considering her indolence, that she had so many friends. Well, maybe he could understand: she was guileless; she harboured no ill will. He was sent to the convenience store on Summerhill Avenue for peanuts and chips and mixes. "Not to worry," she assured him, "everyone brings a bottle. All we need are enough clean glasses." He went back and bought five dozen plastic glasses.

Gyorgi dressed for the evening. He wore a white shirt and a patterned silk tie and real gold cufflinks—gifts of grateful women. He looked distinguished, almost, in a suit. The synthetic brown cloth hung on his frame like an admiral's uniform. She introduced him: "Isn't he gorgeous!" He walked behind her and watched gravely while she went about kissing men and "adoring" them. In his turn he was careful not to flirt with women. He could take no chances: women mistook his compliments for confessions.

He assumed the dignity of the foreman he remembered in the Bechstein factory, hands behind his back, observing everyone, recording, alert to what might be expected of him. He mixed drinks, removed coats, and carried them upstairs; clipped pairs of galoshes and boots together with clothespins. After a while he realized that the guests made no distinction between him and themselves. An envoy from India invited him to a cricket match in Edwards Gardens next summer; Gyorgi invited him in return to a soccer match next summer, also in Edwards Gardens. A pretty psychiatrist wept on his breast in revealing an unhappy marriage; he told her of his own two divorces. A stockbroker took him aside, confided that metals were going to be big, and gave him a business card. Gyorgi went upstairs and got his business card, which he gave to the stockbroker. Gyorgi was overcome by a sophistication he had never known before. In his new expansiveness he slid into discussions.

"Hitler never wanted war," he said with the authority of one who also has an inside track to matters of importance, "he waited outside Poland for word from Chamberlain, who double-crossed him and declared war on Germany. The Allies have falsified history. Hitler could have invaded Britain but ordered the generals to hold off, always hoping for peace. The Holocaust was a lie, spread by Jewish international bankers."

She, meanwhile, had been circling. In the silence that followed his revelations she linked her arm through his and pulled him away just when he was about to heap fact upon startling fact. Tomorrow (he intends) he will tell her: "It is not respectful for a woman to interrupt a man when he is speaking. You must never do that again."

Instead, it was she who faced him when everyone had gone. She was calm; there was a hardness about her as she stood looking up at him without a flicker or a twinge: "You must never, never again reveal your fascism. I will not permit racist talk in my house."

*

When the spring sun began to stream through the shiny windows and the lawn gave off a yielding odour, Gyorgi, too, softened. He permitted her to sing for him in the evening, to wear costumes and a little make-up. She accompanied herself at the Bechstein, the rings on both hands flashing under the crystal lights. He listened to her stories of the operas, stories of terror and love and irony and death. He listened and planned. There would be the garden to attend to, storms to be taken down, screens to be installed, dining room chairs to be repaired. Days of work; music and parties; nights of love. The picture of an old woman dying and leaving him her big house faded, then disappeared altogether.

This night she was dressed as Mimi, looking quite appealing, he thought, in a pink bonnet tied with satin ribbons under her chin. She looked girlish and demure. He even recognized the song in which Mimi asks for a muff to warm her poor, cold hands. Suddenly she broke off, rose abruptly from the piano, turned off the lights, lit acandle, and waving it high overhead, announced:

"I want to die slowly like Mimi." She placed the candle on the table at the side of his chair and sank at his feet. "Do you still want to marry me?"

"Marry me . . . ?" Gyorgi repeated, and his voice broke. He saw himself answering the ring at the front door, raising his eyebrows, and, if necessary, directing the caller to the servants' entrance. Forgiveness flowed over him. In his mind he sent money to his mother and father to come for a visit to see what he had made of himself. Then would come his brothers and sisters, each in turn. He drew her up on his lap. He removed Mimi's bonnet and stroked her head.

She, dreaming: "I feel like Gretel," cradling into him, "we will be like Hansel and Gretel, alone in the forest. We will learn to live in innocence, like peasants, gathering nuts and berries, protected from evil by our happiness."

"You people," he said, shaking his head, "I love the way you people want to play poor, with your budgets and your diets, with your gurus and your torn jeans." Suddenly he became angry. "It is all one big lie: you people couldn't survive a day's hunger."

"I'm not pretending. When I marry, Oswald cuts off my alimony. This is his house, lock, stock, and four-poster. We will not be allowed to stay here." Her teeth were clamped together. "Oswald would never let us live in his house."

Gyorgi felt evicted, dislodged from a place in his head. Somehow he did not find it odd that he should be striking out at her. But she was off his lap and out of range with a swiftness that surprised him: she must have expected something like this.

"You tricked me!" he shouted. "The work ... the hours ... I cleaned up your bloody mess ... it was to have been for me, for me, damn you ... all this time I was busting my ass for him ... for *his* house ... "

In his fury he lunged at her. She ran from him and he after her with fists extended. His anger also brought confusion: images of her friends, lawyers and judges and others in high places before whom he was powerless: he could smell the acid of a jail cell. He heard a crash. He stopped in his tracks as if shot and he heard her laugh. She was standing with her back to the Bechstein, her rump on the keys, her arms flung out and back in a posture of protection. He was astounded that she knew so little about him after all these days and nights that she could think him capable of harming a Bechstein. He banged his knuckles against each other and did not touch her. He opened his fingers and let his arms hang.

"What will become of you?" she taunted "You have been spoiled, spoiled by mahogany and fine linen and oil paintings on the walls. You are unfit now for rented rooms and tired waitresses and the hopes of check-out girls."

So. They had come to the end of the game. It made him sad; he had liked her: he could have been satisfied. Then, doglike, shaking the discovery off himself, he withdrew, walking backwards. Gyorgi kept going, backwards, stepping over the thick carpets for the last time.

*

Where she is standing, in her shabby Mimi gown, arms still extended against her beloved piano, dry-eyed, ears strained towards the sounds of Gyorgi's departure, she knows already she will soon sit across the desk from fair, florid Oswald. She hears already his instructions: no calls. Hears Oswald's voice without a rise in it saying: "What happened this time? Hmm. You got off easy. Give me the account." She knows, too, that Oswald will lace his pale fingers across his chest and quote for the hundredth time: " 'Even among galley slaves there were ten percent volunteers.' For God's sake, when will you stop inviting your own destruction." She sees already her hungry hand as it moves across the desk. She will take the money to keep her safe for yet another little while.

SURPRISE!

Sonja Ferguson believed that the great sin in marriage is not adultery but boredom. Lassitude, she thought, is more dangerous than lust. She made a ritual of avoiding what she deemed to be the ordinary, the predictable, or the merely dull habits of cohabitation. She was a daughter of immigrant Polish Jews; her husband, a descendent of Mayflower-type Presbyterians. These facts in themselves would suggest a degree of challenge, but Sonja kept looking for novelty. There were constant ceremonials, elaborately managed, which, somehow, misfired. Arthur did not exactly respond with wild delight at his wife's attempts to create gay little diversions; at best he remained patient.

For instance: each time Arthur went away on a trip (he was very much in demand on panel discussions on "The Arts Today"), Sonja devised some special greeting for his homecoming. Once, at Christmas time, he returned to find three black young men from the African Students' League. They were polite, intelligent lads, who, for two entire weeks, charmed his wife and delighted the children. But Arthur couldn't work on his new book, "Whither the Intellectual," during this valuable holiday period. The unaccustomed household sounds, the strange outbursts of laughter that exploded like firecrackers outside his door, impinged on his mind, splintering his thoughts. Moreover, it was the first time in his life that Arthur missed Christmas dinner in Fergus, Ontario, where he was born and where his parents still lived. After the foreign guests left, and the unproductive holidays were over, Arthur explained to Sonja that Christmas, traditionally, is a time best spent with one's own family.

Yet again, with the simple faith of one who is herself unable to keep to a schedule, Sonja trusted that the plane bearing her husband would land on time, even if it was February and storming outside. She planned to surprise him with a birthday party. When Arthur did not show up, Sonja and her friends shouted "Surprise!" at approximately the right time, blew out 42 candles and offered up toast after toast to the jolly, albeit absent, good fellow. "To Arthur!" they shouted over and over as they raised their glasses. By the time Arthur did get home in the small blizzarding hours, only his three children, sailing ice-cubes in the three kitchen sinks, heard the doorbell. At some point later, these same children politely waited for their mother to finish a number of frenzied telephone calls, to tell her it was all right—Daddy was upstairs, asleep.

One fine spring day Sonja was awaiting Arthur's return from Montreal. He had been away for ten days organizing and lecturing at a Conference of the Arts. He was due back in about an hour. It had been very warm and humid, rare indeed for early May in Toronto. This time, with conscious restraint, she had done nothing out of the ordinary. A cold supper was ready and a crystal jug of martinis was sweating in the fridge. Altogether a simple, uncomplicated situation. Perhaps, though, she ought to mark the occasion by just dressing up a little. She considered a black chiffon, strapless and almost backless, which she had worn only once, three years ago. Arthur had not liked that dress. "You look different," had been his comment. "In what way?" "Well—I don't know—not like—just different." "Different from what?" she had persisted. "Well, not like the sweet girl I married." Now be a good sport, old girl, she told herself, don't be an image pooper. Be a sweet girl, a nice girl, a true blue, pip, pip and all that girl. Cover up, tone down and disappear. Such bitterness over a mere choice of dress was a warning: an old feeling of loss was always there, just waiting to seize her. Sonja left the bedroom quickly.

Just in time she remembered she hadn't finished clipping the newspaper reports on the Conference. Arthur will sort them and she will paste them in his scrap book. Her mind picked here and there as she cut the newsprint. She lined up her questions. Her husband was a taciturn man who needed to be drawn out, to be interviewed. Interviewed? She couldn't think of another word to describe the questions, hers, the answers, his, that formed their conversations. She had read somewhere that writers do not like to talk much, that they are reluctant to give voice to thoughts lest they lose them. By asking the right questions, Sonja encouraged her husband to speak to her. They always talked about him and his work. Arthur would unwind his information slowly, sometimes snipping the gray yarn unexpectedly, as if he had measured out enough. Yet, should she try to pick up the thread during a pause, he would disregard her words and start up where he had left off, his voice trampling over hers. The result was always a *monologue à deux*. Slowly she gave way to a familiar despondency, a self-pity, which shrank her spirit. She tried not to swallow the gritty ash: there you go, she told herself, being Jewish again. Then, Sonja wondered, what do I mean, being Jewish. I suppose, she thought, it is my father, always complaining, helplessly; it is my mother, sharp in reply, with words sharp as kitchen knives. It is this need to denigrate what is beyond one's control. What could not be helped was to be despised.

SURPRISE!

By the time Arthur's key clicked in the lock, Sonja was well into the martinis. She was wearing the black chiffon dress.

"Hail the hero!" she greeted her husband. Arthur stood in the doorway in triplicate. Sonja blinked hard, then shut her eyes. She never could hold her liquor. When she was able to focus she saw him standing, puzzled and uncertain, as if he had come to the wrong house. At his side was a couple, a man and a woman, smiling at her. Arthur began, "May I introduce—" but Sonja, still unsteady, interrupted, "So look who's here. A delegation yet. With whom have I the pleasure? Pardon me, wrong role. Mustn't remind me of me. Where's Mrs. Ferguson? Ah, here I am. Now then. How do you do. Charmed, I'm sure. Won't you come in. You too, Mr. Ferguson, Sir." Arthur attempted a smile, but his brows met instead.

"Hello, Sonja," said the man.

"Hi, Issy."

"It's Irwin now," Issy said. "I think you know my wife."

"Fanny?"

"Francine."

Sonja began to giggle, then the three burst into laughter. They looked guilty, as if in collusion, having indulged in some deception and gotten away with it. Nobody moved. Arthur finally pushed his way past the trio. "Excuse me. Uh. Excuse me. Well, well, small world, imagine you knowing one another, fancy that, small world after all," his hearty tone changing to irritation when he came close to his wife, "really, what's come over you, behave yourself," he whispered at her. Sonja sighed. She must have done something wrong again.

After dinner they sat around the table. The atmosphere had changed: a fresh, dry breeze came from the garden. Arthur was relaxed, his long arms hung loosely over the back of his chair. He joined their laughter over youthful escapades; he matched their stories with his own recollections. All at once Irwin became restless. He shifted uneasily as if he were adrift in an overcrowded rowboat. His stubby fingers kept reaching for articles still on the table, a spoon, matches, crumbs, cigarette butts, anything. Dissatisfied with what he found, he plowed his hands, first one, then the other, through his thick black hair. He used to be so placid, Sonja thought. But maybe it was just an impression he chose to give, because fat people are supposed to be good-natured.

"Irwin hates to leave his typewriter," Francine said. "Imagine, he didn't want to go to the Conference, not even with everything paid for. But I made him go anyway." She turned toward Arthur. "I wish Irwin would get a job at a university, like you. He won't even apply. He says if they want him, they know where to find him. Some attitude!"

Arthur replied that there is great security in a teaching post. "A writer must come out of his ivory tower. I made several good contacts. There were people up from the States, including publishers. The man from Macmillan's spoke to me about paperbacks. I also lined up some talks for the CBC. It all adds up, you know."

Francine knew. They continued: statement and confirmation. In flat marketplace voices they put their practicalities out in the open.

Irwin turned to Sonja. "Your husband is teaching my wife a few angles she has overlooked. I don't mind, though, someone has to think about the rent."

Sonja smiled into his gleaming glasses. She was full of understanding. They would have a little chat, quietly, like they used to in his father's old car. Irwin now was in a gentle mood. There was about him an aura of resignation without bitterness, which she associated with bearded men at prayers in the synagogue.

"Do you have any children?" she asked.

"Four. All girls. Imagine me a hero to four little females. How about you?"

"Two boys and a girl."

"Where are the children? I haven't seen them."

"At my sister-in-law's. I sent them there until tomorrow. It gives Arthur and me a chance for an uninterrupted evening together. Children can be so demanding that there is danger of losing touch with the fundamental relationship between husband and wife."

"What rot! Children *are* the marriage. You sound like a sink-side psychologist. Relationships yet!"

"You left your children."

"That's different. I don't send them away from their own home as some kind of a nuisance. Anyway, their adoring, indulgent, maternal grandmother is taking care of the girls while we are away."

"How is your new book coming along?" Sonja asked.

"Hold on, wait a minute. You're changing the subject. What did I say, what was the key word? Grandmother? Aha, I'm right. How is your mother, and your father?"

"All right, I guess."

"Still having trouble?"

"Had. It's been ten years since they spoke to me."

"I'm sorry. That's a shame. I don't suppose they took kindly to your marrying Arthur. They would think of him as a 'goy'. Is that it?"

Sonja felt it was none of his business. But one must not be rude to a guest. Moreover, she realized that Irwin was one of those people who had never learned to make indifferent talk, a kind of careful non-talk that avoids intimacy. She tried a flippant tone: "Disowned. Dead. Sackcloth and ashes. They did the only decent thing under the circumstances—they moved to Los Angeles. They left me to my well-deserved fate, left me with what they called that 'bunch of cold fish.' Really, Issy, I didn't expect them to approve, or even to understand, but when the children were born, I did hope . . . "

Thought trails away into emptiness. How quickly the round gives way when memory is the gravedigger.

"Perhaps your parents felt you wouldn't be happy," Irwin was saying, "and maybe it was hard for them to stand by and watch. Just a guess." He found a pipe in a pocket and became very busy with it, filling, packing, lighting, puffing, puffing, as if his life depended on that piece of wood.

"Then they were wrong. I am perfectly happy. Perfectly," she protested, if not too much, certainly too loud. Arthur and Francine looked up from their bookkeeping. Sonja lowered her voice. "Still, to ignore their only grandchildren—" She must talk to someone. "I don't know if you remember the time my brother was killed," she began. The pipe was trembling in Irwin's hand and she sensed that the past was knocking him about, too. It was no use, he didn't hear her, he was listening to himself. Issy, like everyone else, had abandoned her. The hand she hoped to clasp was being put to better use, digging in a tobacco pouch. She was on her own again, alone, her arms flailing the empty air, like an infant suddenly bereft of its swaddling clothes.

"Glad to hear that," Irwin said. He had heard nothing past the point of her being happy. So be it. "Then you and your husband get along pretty well?" he went on.

"Of course. Why shouldn't we."

"Well, after all, you were brought up with a different set of ground rules. Sometimes when Fran and I have a fight, the insults are so absurd in translation, we die laughing instead."

"I find that sort of thing primitive. After all, one must behave like a rational human being."

"You never quarrel?"

"Never."

"Somehow, I never thought you were the type."

"What type?"

"Phony. Wasteland in the bedroom."

"You've got a nerve!"

He laughed. "Watch out, your rational is slipping."

Sonja dared not reply: he was baiting her; she must control herself. She turned away and looked at Arthur, to comfort herself with his blond good looks, to remind herself of her own husband's steady, even ways; to lean, as it were, against his broad, upright back. The hum of voices ceased and there was a sudden uneasiness. All four looked at one another and away again.

"We really must be going," Francine said, "it was a real pleasure."

"I'll mail you a copy of my new book when it comes out," Arthur said.

Irwin rose abruptly and headed for the hall, opened the door, said, "Autographed, of course," and was gone, without another word.

"Of course," Arthur replied, pleasantly, missing the sarcasm, but Irwin didn't hear. He was moving so fast down the street on his small, round feet that Francine had to run to catch up with him.

"Well, well," Arthur said to Sonja, "what a real surprise. Imagine you people all knowing one another. I thought you would like them, that's why I asked them to drive in with me from the airport. To think you had actually gone to school together! Small world, eh? He's a bit strange, but talented, I think. Pretty woman, his wife, all there," tapping his forehead, "solid." He loosened his tie. "Gad, it's hot." And started up the stairs; Sonja followed.

"Arthur," she said, "you haven't asked about the kids, you haven't even thought I bet about your children."

Without turning, he asked, "They're all right, aren't

they?" and kept going, as if the question contained its own affirmative answer.

Sonja slid past him on the stairs and faced him from a step above his.

"They're all right, aren't they?" he repeated.

She remained unmoving in front of him, barring his ascent.

"Oh sure. But I want them home tonight. I want to see them, right now, this very minute. Come on, Art, let's go pick them up. It would be a lovely surprise."

"I'm in no mood for kids and surprises. Honey, I'm dead beat. What I need is a shower and a good sleep."

"Please, Art, come with me now to pick them up. Together." She had her hands on his upper arms as if to turn him around. "Don't you see, they're not expecting us, and having us arrive when they're asleep, waking them up, carrying them home in their pyjamas, why, what a surprise it would be, they would just adore it."

"Sonja, be reasonable. I'm so tired. We'll go first thing in the morning. I promise."

"What kind of a father are you anyway!" It was her mother's voice, high-pitched and whining. "You don't want to see your own children!"

Arthur, like his father, wiped his face clean of any expression. He made no reply. He tried to swing his arms free. But she shifted quickly, and with both palms against his chest she pushed so hard, he was forced to grab at the bannister to keep from falling backwards. His calmness wavered. Then, maneuvering past her, he ran up the remaining steps, straight into the bathroom and by slamming the door, locked himself in.

"That's a stupid stunt, a coward's trick," she screamed.

With a pin from her hair she slipped the lock and flung open the bathroom door. She confronted him with her presence. He would not look at her. He was just seated on the toilet, taking off his shoes. For just a second she wanted to laugh: there was something idiotic about the way she stood over him, agitated and angry, interfering with her husband's simple desire to take a shower.

"I'm fed up," she shouted. The acoustics in a bathroom are excellent. She rather enjoyed the way her voice reverberated. "Fed up with running a private hotel for you. Whether you like it or not, you are married and the father of three children, all widowed and orphaned before their time. Big deal, all this gratuitous chairmanship. Anyway, how you can stomach all that creamed chicken, I'll never understand."

"At least they don't put garlic in it." His head was lowered as he unbuttoned his shirt. "I'm scared to eat a boiled egg around here in case you've stuffed it with garlic."

"Then you'd better keep going 'round the chicken patty circuit. Everything is going to get spicier around here."

"Be a good girl," he begged, "and let me have my shower first."

He threw the shirt on top of the laundry hamper. Sonja automatically lifted the lid and placed the shirt inside. She watched him undress. He handed her the underwear which she put away. He opened the door for her, but she wouldn't move.

"Your shower, your trips, your time-table, your schedules, your everything!" She kicked the door shut again, and the sound of the slam was the sound of trumpets. Sonja was ready to charge.

"What the devil has gotten into you?" Arthur demanded, "it was your idea to park the kids at Lucille's. They get in your way, not mine."

"Of course not. You're never home long enough for anyone to get in your way. And when you *are* home, you might as well not be here. You're locked in that precious study of yours, in that holy of holies. I'm warning you, I'm going to invade your exclusive little world, your tight little island, your self-contained, restricted, no-Jews-allowed, private club, membership of one."

"Oh no, not that old stuff. Just because I don't like garlic, I am accused of anti-Semitism."

"That's not funny; I'm not joking. I can't bear it—this always being on the outside. Do you take me for one of your pioneer women, out in the wilderness, tending the hearth in a log cabin, while you're trading with the Indians? Before I'm through you'll have nothing left to trade with!"

She seized his new wrist-watch lying on the window sill and flung it into space. The gold glittered in the air for an instant before it disappeared. "Now you'll have to find the time!" Like a beachcomber, she pounced on the next find: a large brown brogue. She threw it out, then did the same with its mate. "Never drop just one shoe." She looked wildly about, then lifted his trousers off the hook. She made a shapeless bundle of his pants before she tossed them out. "Never anything worthwhile in your pants anyway." Arthur, in his socks, was mesmerized. His wife stood like a termagant, fists clenched, elated and tense, waiting for him to come to. It didn't take long.

"You little bitch!" his voice in low key.

They faced one another, embattled.

"You damned bitch!" he repeated, louder, with more assurance.

With one strong hand he gripped her wrists and held them in a vise behind her back; he pushed her towards the shower stall with his free hand. Her struggle was mere reflex: the force of his arms was irresistible: her senses, surprised, betrayed her: she forgot what it was she was angry about. She was under the shower, shocked by cold water. Gasping. "My good dress—my shoes—Arthur, please—"

"This should cool you off," Arthur said.

Sonja couldn't move because of the tight hold he kept on her. Nor did she want to. He was under the icy torrent with her, his chest hard against her breasts.

"Are you going to behave?" her husband demanded.

"I promise. Just make the water a little warmer."

L'ENVOI

... Tell me, father, what I did wrong and I will never do it again ...

The young girl seated on the cart beside the pedlar, or, perhaps behind him on top of whatever goods he was carrying—that nine-year old girl must have had such a thought, not concretely, for the young are protected from premature awareness. It can be assumed that her mind was dealing with everything or with nothing as a result of confusion as she looked up at her father's pock-marked, bearded face. Then the pedlar brought the birch switch down on the horse and the cart rumbled off.

The girl did not know then, nor could she ever say, why she was sent away to live in a distant city amongst strangers. That day in 1912 she was sent to Lublin to live with her grandmother. Whose mother, her mother's or her father's? She never explained: it was as if the details of the transitions in her life were of no significance: one was born in this or that place, into this or that family, poor or poorer, one prevailed or one died.

Nor did she ever recall whether she left in the dead of winter, when hunger and cold were at their most abysmal; or whether it was in the heat of summer, when the wells dried up and the dirt streets gave off a dust one tasted; or if it was in a season in between. They drove off very early in the morning, probably, to get a good start on the day since the pedlar would be making many stops at farmhouses and small villages to sell whatever it was he had in the back of the cart—pots, pans, linens, shoes and hats. Perhaps the sun was shining.

She was sent away from her home in Radom in Poland. Home consisted of two rooms, dark and dank, with an earthen floor. The ears always strained for the clang of horses' hooves. The terror of an unsheathed sword. A sound in the night of a stumbling, drunken peasant, demanding money and jewels that "every dirty Jew has hidden." Wakefulness induced by bedbugs. Vermin. Sores that would not heal. Sudden death. (I know, because I was born in that same place years later.) Memory, too, must have suffered indignities for she could remember nothing of the journey. If no one told her why she was being sent away from her mother, father, two brothers and three sisters, then she was forced to exist without the memory of words. Something should have been said—the truth, a lie, an approximation even—for in the absence of words a presence slips in to fill the emptiness and haunts forever.

Scenes of preparation for leaving home can be imagined. For weeks her head had been doused with kerosene to kill lice. Her brothers and sisters, sensing something portentous going on, watch covertly. Her gentle small mother (from a faded sepia photograph) kneels on the floor to bathe her eldest daughter the night before. The water is in a tin tub on the floor. The mother frequently raises a wrist to adjust a shabby, brown wig that keeps slipping over her eyes as she bends over her child's body. The girl's one dress is clean. Perhaps shoes are found for the journey. And her father, tall and handsome, his face turned to the wall in a corner of the same room, phylacteries wound about his arm, fingers the fringes of a prayer shawl and remains deep in a dialogue with God.

(I remember my grandfather always, it seemed to me, at prayer, intoning litanies, stroking his beard and swaying as he prayed. Otherwise, he was silent, a man distanced by futility and religion.)

Surely, as a final paternal gesture the girl's father held her, even if only to help her up on the seat. Surely he said something to his friend, the pedlar. For the man who bore the child away was not a stranger. He was her father's best friend. They had been friends since boyhood, having studied at the *Yeshivah* together. As young men, in order to avoid military service, they had administered to one another the blows that broke the bones of the index finger of the right hand. The pedlar, seated with the reins in his hands, assured his dearest friend that he would take good care of the child and deliver her safely to her widowed grandmother.

At the last moment the father no doubt spoke:

"Be good. Listen to your grandmother."

She kept her eyes on her father's face, photographing the high forehead, straight brows, the skin ravaged by small pox, the beard thick and black. The girl must have felt an urge to run and scream, but the passivity required of her at that moment was fixed forever. At that moment, also a volcanic energy was born, hidden from sight, seething with a fiery rage, to erupt without warning throughout her lifetime.

*

I suppose Julius will always be nervous at a preview opening of an exhibit. Tonight, at his sixth one-man show, he has been backed into a corner at the far end of the gallery, between two of his canvases; he looks pale and ill at ease. The Gallery Donegani is very long and very narrow and it is impossible to step back from a painting without colliding with someone who is also stepping back from a painting on the wall opposite. To view the exhibit, people soon learn to move to the right only, sideways. Earlier, Julius was interviewed by a tv reporter and was centered for a few minutes under the tv camera lights. All this time I have been standing firmly to the right of the open doorway, brushed against but not disturbed. A few people recognize me as Julius' wife, but since the wine has been set out at the other end, they do not linger.

Everyone we know or have ever known (except Jim, who couldn't make it, but sent a wire of congratulations) has come to the opening. Julius is in that fortunate position, creatively speaking, where his artistic growth is at the exact meeting point with the public's recognition of his work. And while I am pleased that Julius no longer has to suffer anonymity, I cannot help but worry how long do an artist and his public stay at this meeting point? Who goes on to by-pass the other? Julius is clasping and unclasping his hands like parting lovers. I think he would feel more comfortable if he had something in his hands. His hands seem to have a will of their own; he satisfies them by giving them brushes to hold, paint to mix. During the night, in his sleep, his hands clutch the pillow's edge, a sheet, a blanket.

I am drunk, lonely and desperate. It is on such occasions, when I should be self-contained with pleasure, that a perversity takes hold and I keep drinking the cheap wine, and I say to the nice young man who has been very attentive and has brought me glass after glass; and who, moreover, is asking *my* opinion—it is at times like these that I hold forth and say,

"Control? Oh yes. You are indeed perceptive to have discovered Julius' tremendous control over his work: control over his ideas, over form, over content, over technique. Total control. Yes, indeed, most amazing. But," I whisper confidentially, "nature punishes over-specialization by giving the organism what it wants. Consider the oyster. It can survive only within a certain range of temperature and degree of salinity in the water and depends on the food passing by. This controls the entire future of the species, because once he's attached to his culch, the oyster cannot move an inch. Where," I ask earnestly, "where will all this control lead?"

The new art critic for the *Toronto Planet* (it was) appropriated my casual remarks as his own considered critical opinion. Julius raged. "That man is stupid . . . the fool . . . he missed the whole point . . . there's no such thing as 'too controlled' for God's sake . . . might as well call my work too artistic . . . the idiot doesn't know that control is crucial to all great art goddamnit . . . "

*

For a short while after the exhibit Julius' hands held me at night and we became as we had been once. Then he began to work in his studio again and forgot everything. He forgot the show's success, the amount of money that was coming; he forgot *The Planet*'s art critic; and he forgot me. More than once he has told me that "an artist must forget; he must have no memory." Memory, I suppose, can be disturbing, since memory and emotion often go together, sometimes to no apparent purpose, so why permit memories to intrude on one's life . . . ? So I surmised.

Then Julius picked up his paint brushes again in the day and clutched the bedding at night. Familiar life was resumed, which included a visit from Jim, my husband's best friend. Their bonding, as that kind of close tie is termed nowadays, goes back to childhood, through all the rites of passage. The fact that Jim and I are lovers has not affected their friendship.

At two on Friday afternoon I picked up Jim at the airport, drove to his hotel, we made love until six and then I drove him to our house for dinner. The traffic crawled at that hour and we had time to catch up on the lives of our children since he was here almost six months ago. I have two grown sons who call him Uncle Jim; he has eight children whom I have seen only in snapshots, living as they do in the three American cities where their mothers' divorces were granted. In front of my house, before we got out of the car, Jim cautioned, as he always does:

"We mustn't do anything to hurt Julius."

When Jim comes into town he and Julius are together as much as possible. Even when the three of us are in our car, Julius and Jim sit side by side in the front and I sit in the back. My affair with Jim is more a matter of propinquity than of passion. We three are such good friends that sometimes I imagine myself as Jeanne Moreau, loved by Jules *et* Jim.

*

Every summer Julius leaves his third floor studio and sets up his work in the living room, which also faces north. Each summer we are thrown together a great deal in that part of the house I consider mine. It is becoming difficult to share space with my husband. To make matters worse, instead of going about my daily routines, I find myself hanging about while he paints. He has grown a beard. "Don't hide your face, I love every mark on it," I used to plead whenever, in the past, he wanted to grow a beard as other painters did. "Every scar makes me think of ordeals and victories." "Aw, come on, it was only a bad case of adolescent acne." But just the same he was pleased and took a shave.

I spend hours watching Julius as he contemplates a canvas on the wall before him; he holds the brushes in one hand and strokes his beard with the other. I have not been able to take my eyes off the beard and the pocked skin above it. All summer long I have been watching the beard grow, as it went from a bluish skid-row shadow, to a black stubble that Julius dug his fingers into constantly, then to its ultimate thick blackness which is in strange contrast with his thinning brownish hair. I worried about the bare patches just under the lower lip; then, with relief, I saw the bald spots fill in with soft hairs. Here and there at the edges, especially towards the ears, some gray appeared. It is now September, and Julius is back in his third floor studio, yet I am still not used to the sight of that beard. The worst time is in bed at night when, if his beard brushes against my arm, my face or neck, my skin shrivels.

"Jim is coming today. He's going to stay here."

"Great!" Julius said. "I've got four new pictures to show him."

"He's not coming on business, nor to see you—he's coming to see *me*."

"What exactly does that mean?"

"It means that I phoned him to come right away. I must talk to him." In the absence of a response, I added. "I've got to talk to someone; I can't stand it any more."

" 'It' again. What is 'it' this time?"

"Your beard. I hate it. I wish you'd shave it off."

In his silence I heard: "And then what? If I give in to you again, you will be satisfied for a while, I will work, you will keep busy; then for no reason you will get bitchy and I will have to stay out of your way, especially in bed."

Behind his departing back I hurled my silent reply, "Since you refuse to talk to me openly so that together we might make a discovery of some sort, I shall continue to be unfaithful to you. You might as well know that in a scale of one to ten, Jim is eleven in bed: *you* are about four and half."

Either Julius did not know or he did not want to know that in the middle of the night I left our bed. For the rest of that night I lay beside Jim in the spare bedroom. Jim knows a great deal about women, about their "needs," which is his term for that impossible longing for intimacy.

"You must understand that Julius loves you," he assured me, "it's just that he can't turn off his creativity."

"I'm with him all the time too, and he can turn me off very easily."

Jim embraced me. It is his way of saying, "Now, be reasonable . . . "

The three of us had breakfast together as if nothing had happened in the night. I looked closely at my husband to see how he had slept, but neither his eyes nor his expression showed signs of suffering. After the third cup of coffee, the two men rose and went up to the studio. Jim carried a case of beer. Late in the afternoon Jim came down into the kitchen. He stood beside me at the sink, serious, concentrating on the potato peels.

"Julius asked me to tell you that he will give you $50,000 and 10 percent of all his future sales if you'll get out." Now he was watchful and stood well back of the knife in my hand. "His words, not mine."

"Julius hasn't got $50,000. He's just starting to sell. That's your money he's offering me."

"He's my best friend."

"You're *my* best lover."

"I feel like a flea between two pit terriers."

"Tell me what I have done wrong that he wants to send me away."

"He feels that in some way you are undermining him. Julius says he can't paint. He has to work. It's as simple as that. Oh come on . . . it's not the end of the world . . . you need to live your own life . . . maybe this will be for the best . . . think about it."

"There's nothing to think about. This is my home. He can't make me leave."

Suddenly I was overcome by the recurrence of an old dread, a mysterious anguish that paralyzes me. Jim took the knife out of my hand. He made me sit down. He drew up another chair so close to mine that his long legs were on either side of my chair. He took both of my hands in his and held them between his thighs.

"My entire life," I said, "my entire life has been spent trying to forge one human tie with one person in this whole wide world who would want me."

I had just begun. Injustice, humiliation, overweening desires—I opened a bin of unclaimed emotions. Jim let go of me. He was curt.

"Keep it light. Keep it light. Let's not get serious."

"Jim," I told him, "deep down you're shallow."

In the narrowing of his eyes I saw already the determination of a man hardened by many partings.

Out of habit I served dinner and out of habit Julius and Jim sat down to eat. I broke the silence. I turned to Jim:

"You've always liked Julius' work, haven't you?"

"Oh yes, right from the start when we were students at the Ontario College of Art. Everyone recognized he was the real thing, the born painter; the teachers left him alone."

"Then why," I asked, my tone silken, "do you, as the great international art consultant, choose all that crap that goes into lobbies of skyscrapers and all that mediocrity hanging on the walls of executive offices? You have never bought one of Julius' paintings."

"Oh, those people . . . ! They're not ready for experiments."

All this time my husband was abstracted, hardly listening. Now he looked up, as if he had just thought of something:

" . . . you never asked me to submit anything . . . "

Jim said, "Don't you see what she's doing . . . divide and rule . . . "

I said, "Don't you see what *he's* been doing? He picks your brains. He finds out what you dismiss as suitable only for motels and *buys* it! He peddles paintings as if they were pots and pans. He's nothing but a pedlar."

Jim got up to leave. The way he looked at Julius, the way his hands went up into the air and then disappeared into his pockets, left me with a final image of a drowning man just before he goes under for the last time.

Every morning now I am up early to prepare a substantial breakfast for my husband. Then Julius leaves for the studio loft on King Street that I found for him. I've not seen what he's been working on. At breakfast we listen to the radio news; we share the morning paper; we have our old desultory chats about matters which do not directly concern us.

"Are you interested in seeing the van Gogh exhibit," I ask, "if I can wangle a couple of tickets?"

"Well . . ."

"It's all right. I just wondered. What are you working on these days?"

" 'Breakfast Number Four.' "

"Seriously . . ."

"Seriously."

"Abstract expressionism . . . ?"

"Something. Walter was over yesterday. He likes the new series. Wants a show next year."

"You can use the house this weekend, if you want to. I'll be away."

"Well . . . it means dragging things back and forth. Maybe some sketches." He puts down the paper. "Artists and intellectuals are not safe in this world."

"I know a man who is an authority on Russian military history."

"Listen, if you get a chance, will you check our account at the bank. Maybe I ought to open my own account near the studio. There's a branch at Bathurst and Queen."

"Leave it. They know us here and will cover if we overdraw."

"All right. See you at six."

We go out into the hall together. In the winter I wait until he puts on overshoes and hat and scarf and overcoat. Sometimes he takes a lunch and I carry it to the front door. Then we have a parting kiss; I am getting used to the feel of his beard.

Julius leaves and I go into the living room, the curtains are sheer and although I can see out, no one can see me from the street. As the days and months go by I keep a morning watch at the window. I watch as Julius crosses the road and then stands on the sidewalk opposite and looks up at his former studio. I observe that his beard is short and neat and his moustache is trimmed, giving him the look of a French *boulevardier*. I wait until he is out sight, then I start the day.

A VIEW FROM THE ROOF

In Old San Juan in the Hotel El Convento once long ago a convent, the nuns' burial ground now a patio with bar and swimming pool, an where, the first night, Sunday, the delegates met and sat: six pale Canadians, upright and winter-weary, opposite six from Latin America. Their (Latin) men being dark and deferential and their women pigeon-breasted and charming, and all well (English) spoken. From Toronto, Bernard Adelman, true to his name, meaning in translation from Yiddish, a delicate, a gentle man; being tall, with a back rounded by constraint. Betty, his dark short wife, immediately overcome by the tropics, wept for the little Carmelite nuns buried beneath the flagstones under her chair; little martyrs who would no longer feel the hot trade winds and whose agony of a flesh moist under arms and breasts surely had never need of further mortification. Betty and Bernie, tacitly as it happens after twenty years of inexorable proximity, agreed to be titillated, if not any more by each other, at least by the sexes opposite. Potent rum punches until two in the morning and extra tips on the expense account for the tired waiters, whose indifference to the full moon caused perverse determination to linger as long as possible.

Finally upstairs, Bernie, full of pride and position established in the exchange of academic credentials downstairs, turned the key in the heavy dark carved door, number 414. The room in gloom: a sweet mustiness redolent of sea and soap. Betty wondered, I wonder if this was one of their cells, was it the same number 414 then, imagine being locked up like prisoners; imagine; because Betty knew very little about religions, not even about the comparative kind, her father having been a communist who had warned her about the opiate or was it the opium of the people. Bernie opened the shuttered doors at the other end of the room and called her, but not by name, Hey, look, we have a balcony, come and see. Betty did as expected and he put an arm around his wife: Look, that's the Atlantic out there, see the lights on the boats. While Bernie looked at the boats, Betty turned her head in the opposite direction, to her right, looking at roof-tops clearly visible in the bright night and seeming to be square little gardens of cement, with little chimneys sprouting like bushes; down below them, the street, narrow as an alley, was empty. If he would only take his hand away, if he would remove the weight from her shoulders, if he would only let go of her, she could leap off the balcony across the slit of an abyss and when last seen, why she was right here a moment ago, the children would go about their future, remembering her, for what? correcting their grammar, hot chocolate on cold nights? but she would never forget them wherever she landed.

Let's get out, let's go and see the town, I can hardly wait, Betty said.

Lots of time for sight-seeing. Bernie closing the shutters against the spacious night, it's too late to go out. You heard Mr. Tomas warn us against being out late at night? He especially said not to let you go out at night unescorted; American women think they can do anything. (Actually his words were, the American ladies are so trusting.)

Oh come on now we're safer here than on Yonge Street on Saturday night; didn't you notice, couldn't you positively feel how kind everyone is, and so polite, I'm sure they'd ask permission, so rape is out of the question.

I'm serious.

So am I.

Forget it; we're not leaving here in the middle of the night; don't you understand, we're in an age of revolutionary transitions, these are changing times, traditions are being destroyed, that's why we've come here for the Conference on Education in the Americas; continuing, as if on a platform, there are many irreconcilable elements leading to sporadic outbursts of irrational violence.

All I wanted was to go out for a walk.

She, put off by her husband's refusal to play her game of devious association, called free by psychiatrists, their mothers having taught them the technique in the crib, in order that he (Bernie-man) discover what she (Betty-woman) was hinting at; and in a flash of insight he would make his move, preferably aphrodisiac in nature, which he never did. She, miffed, got undressed and put on her pyjamas. An old signal. Tailored pyjamas declaring inviolability.

He, put off by what was to him yet another illogical female impulse, not realizing the years of secret preparation that goes into an apparent whim, also put on his pyjamas, both sections, firmness and finality in the way he pulled tight the drawstring, sending back his answer, a declaration of independence. He switched on the air-conditioner.

Each turned down a heavy brown woven bedspread on a single bed, sitting for a moment on the edge, face to face, looking not at each other, looking around at the heavy dark Spanish furniture, so authentic she was to call it later Inquisition Modern; at the heavy white draperies against the closed shutters; down at the thick brown rug. Jealous nun ghosts, hiding in the dark corners and under their beds. The renaissance of love was not going to be easy in this hotel room.

Tired? he asked.

It's been a long day.

Wake you up later?

If you want to.

She, sleepless beneath the damp sheets. He, waking up later, but not for love, getting up in the dark, finding without hesitation his briefcase on the desk; and the light shining under the closed bathroom door. She knew he was sitting on the toilet seat going over his speech.

While the other wives went to the beach every morning, Betty sat in the Municipal Auditorium, she having oversold Bernie on team spirit and now expected to turn out to all the games. Which she did daily, with absent-minded duty, the way she attended the children's recitals. Here it was even harder to concentrate because of the heat and the soporific whirr of an ineffectual fan. In one ear. An ear-phone reducing dramatic Spanish to dull English (simultaneously) in the other. Soon learning to stay awake by staring with hot eyes at the learned speakers; sizing them up as husbands at the dinner table; undressing them as lovers in bed; like the way she window-shopped on Sunday without the danger of putting herself where her imagination was. In the evening she met the same men at some reception or party and they would shake her hand briefly, although they greeted other women with a dry, discreet kiss upon the cheek. There appeared to be some kind of pecking order in the kissing ceremony. To a delegate from Chile, a poet, with virile gray hair and sad gray eyes, Betty, emboldened by four daiquiris and the impermanence of their relationship, exposed, at a practical angle, namely, upward slightly to the left, her own right cheek. He moved to his right to face her face.

You didn't kiss me, she said, and she intended reproach.

Only with the greatest exercise of the will, the poet replied, and he intended gallantry.

But you kissed the other ladies.

Oh, not *all* the ladies; some like you are forbidden.

Why? Where is the sign on me saying "Verboten"?

It is there just the same. You are from Canada, yes? concentrating on her left breast displaying the copper maple leaf pin recommended by the travel agent. Began to speak French which she didn't understand any more than Spanish, so stood there, sipping her drink, thinking how tight her shoes had become, fixing on his strong white teeth a stare of inattention.

Late, late every night taxied back to the convent-hotel; going through the lobby without stopping, walking in time to the beat of the dance band playing on the old altar, to the elevator, up to room 414. Betty trailed by desires as if by beggar children; shutting the door on her mendicant emotions, to leave them in the corridor to whisper indignantly the rest of the night.

Friday the final (official) night. At the Casa del Arte for the Esso Exhibit of Latin-American Artists. So agitated a crowd she was pushed (easily) into a corner. Betty separated from Bernie and the group. Alone at last. Up against a large canvas painted white, plastered random with globs of gray cement, painted also with yellow enamel, and black, and collages of pages torn from comic books; titled *The Lovers*. She, feeling anonymous therefore free, spoke out loud to the person beside her. I like his conception: lovers black and brown on white and funny all over, lovers are like a riddle. He (it was) replied: crap, it's all a lot of crap, it's all a lot of crap, the whole show is a fake. She, long since accustomed to non-involved platitudes, became excited at the sound of definitive words which evoked her (discarded) proletarian beginnings. She observed. A young man in an old-fashioned, broad-shouldered predominantly green, tweed jacket; there was sweat on his upper lip and in the hollows beneath his eyes. Observing also his skin was the colour of weak tea and his eyes were light, but his hair was a cap of brown wool and his lips broad and thick. Deciding he was a double-distilled descendent of some fatal impact. Feeling guilty that she of all people should have made note of his negro-ness; she especially shouldn't hold consciousness of race, not even in reflection; after all, it always angered her to be categorized as Jewish. After all. She smiled at him with familiarity, assuming a bond. Perhaps she was not much, if at all, younger than his mother. He was kind. Brought her a chair, a drink; another drink; lifted hors d'oeuvres from floating plates like a magician plucking rabbits out of a hat. She was grateful.

Do you live in San Juan, she asked.

Oh yes, not far from your hotel.

She had noticed them, the men on benches at night, tourist-watching, (he?) in the little park in front of the hotel.

He adding, I live here now, but I was born and brought up in New York. I'm an American. Like you.

I'm Canadian.

Same thing. I came back here, strange I should say I came back; in the States I was made to feel Puerto Rican so in a way I came home. To paint. He looked up and around, holding his breath in memory yet avoiding the issue and blaming elsewhere, pinching his nose as if all the pictures in the gallery had been stored in crude oil and still smelled. Claiming, there are only two genuine works of art in the entire exhibit.

Which ones, show me.

Helped her to her feet, took her arm and held it against his tweed (kindly?) to avoid collision, everyone darting this way and that, mysteriously as fish. No one looking at pictures.

Oh but I love these paintings. Betty, loving in passing, I get a real charge when I see the ingenuity, never underestimate human ingenuity, everybody is so inventive these days, no holds barred, anything goes, she enthused, as if she alone represented the positive point of view in a debate on the future of the human race; brightening her eyes and waving her hands, it's so exciting to actually see what has been imagined. Redundant maybe, but not dissimulating, she not having any objection to anarchy so long as it stayed within bounds, framed and hung out of the way on a wall, her father by now disgusted with her decadent bourgeois taste. Show me the ones you like.

In an alcove at the rear of the gallery two pretty pictures in technicolour, tropical flora and fauna, missing only a ribbon to be garlanded. Betty disappointed. So young and so conservative. Perhaps because he had been deprived in Spanish Harlem, poor lad. Poor homeless man. Still, he *felt*, that is the important thing, he *felt* at home on the Island. And she. Where did she feel at home? Marching in Queen's Park blue skirt white middy red tie on the 24th of May *her* Queen's birthday, only one year away from Lublin, Poland, and Ellis Island. Not in Toronto. The roots. Still. She reminded herself (lest we forget) no roots is better than no grave.

Is your work also representational? she asked. To keep him from leaving.

I can paint in any style. What would you like: abstract expressionism, realism, hard-edge, op or pop. Anything I do is better than most of the crap here.

I would like to see your work I have one day left where is your work exhibited, which gallery?

I hold exhibits on my roof I boycott the commercial galleries. I have nothing to do with them, thieves all of them. I sell my pictures privately that way everybody gets a fair deal. If you're really interested, you can pick up a bargain, my studio is not far from your hotel.

The quick brown hand holds a printed business card chest (hers) high. Her back curves into the curve of the alcove. He facing into her face, thin brown wrists on the wall on either side of her head. Light no-color eyes flat into hers. Just like in the movies when The Man is about to promise Love to The Girl (she must remain The Girl throughout the film because she cannot become The Woman until The Man fulfills his promise). And Betty begins to play The Scene, not having done so during adolescence, a sterile period given to grim discussions about fascism with her father. Mauricio (it was) one inch away from touching. She archly arching. Then speaking, stupidly, as if at a faculty wives' tea, reading the wrong scenario:

My entire family is vitally interested in Art she said with a capital A, my three children are encouraged to be creative; my husband feels it is our duty to support the artists of our time.

He puzzling, moved away and looked into the crowd.

Your husband, is he here?

Oh yes, we're both here.

Is that him, that big man coming over, is that your husband? Moving away further.

Not Bernie.

The man from Esso bearing down on them his large head preceding him like an emissary; inserting his corporate self between Betty and Mauricio Sulano, not looking at the young man, saying, (only to her) I've been searching all over for you; we're waiting for you for press photos, you're holding us up. Betty smiled an apology at the young man Mauricio and said she (Mommy?) would be right back. The man from Esso grabbed her elbow, bull-dozed his way through the crowd, holding on to her, but not kindly, so that she tended to hang back, which in turn tightened his grip, which in turn.

They, the rest of the North American contingent, and her husband, all in a huddle but not for pictures, spoke together, where were you what happened to you we were so worried. The women all present and accounted for, virtuously fingering their service-ribbons, displaying gold and diamond combat medals on both hands and wrists. Bernie. Who looked embarrassed. Brought down his sword of disapproval for all to witness his mettle: yes, where the heck have you been, you've made us late for the farewell banquet. Roquero Cordera, anthropology, Panama, kind ancient Inca face you could not help but notice, softly said: my dear lady, we were concerned only for your safety; it is asked merely that you practise caution, one must make allowances for human frailty. The man from Esso nodded his big head, agreeing, that's what I say, he said, you can't be too careful these days, things are changing too fast for comfort.

The end of the Conference. One entire day Saturday free. (Fun?) Let's go to the beach, she said to Bernie, I simply can't go home like this, without even a sunburn. You go to the beach, her husband replied. I must draft my reports while they're still fresh in my mind. Tomorrow. Tomorrow we pack, she told him, the 'plane leaves at two. Well, ha, ha, you can't have everything; me go home heap-big pale face, he laughed. Then seeing her pale face he promised: we'll come back here some day and live it up, we'll lie on the beach, all day; honestly, I promise, now why don't you be a good kid and take the bus with the other girls; have a good time. Betty went. Not on the bus.

Alone, out in the street, out in the sun, in sandals (bare legs), lugging a beach bag, asking and finding the street printed on Mauricio's card. Which way the numbers? They went up-hill and so did she running up the steep hill like a school-girl. Finding his old new-world Spanish house, old plaster patched newly. Door into *chiaroscuro* court-yard, sun stabbing the shadows with shafts of light. Three stories rising on three sides, ringed with two floors of balconies. Silent. Yet the smells of noon cooking. A little girl on the second balcony of the middle building, child and building watching, knowing. The little girl pointed to an entrance at the left. Inside, on the wall at the bottom of a wooden stairway, painted a clear large black cross; on the second landing also a black cross; and on the third; and an arrow pointing to a short ladder. Up the little ladder, through a trap door, onto a flat roof. In the centre a tar-paper shack with tin roof no longer gleaming. Doorless doorway. Mauricio just inside not at all surprised, immediately begins to apologize for the manner in which he is forced to live, a poor roof over his poor head.

It's not much better, he asserts, than New York, except for the weather.

Oh but it's wonderful! You have such freedom.

The freedom to go hungry exists everywhere.

The man from Esso was right. Perhaps not. The paintings were persuasive, she felt drawn to them. To him? Still. Just the same. She took her time. Let me see them all again, she said, from the beginning. He, wordlessly. Both knowing her presence to be some kind of commitment. She procrastinating lest her decision end the . . . . What had she come for? She took out her cheque book. Make it out to cash, he asked. I will, she replied, if you'll take $50. He shrugged and took the cheque: she reached for *Stillborn No. 3*, a convenient size, in deep purple with convoluted black foetuses inside red wombs. He said he would make out a bill of sale so she wouldn't have any trouble at customs. He automatic-writing on a Woolworth pad, giving her the carbon-backed sheet made out at the top to her penny-pinching Rebecca Adelman bank name; his own money-grasping Mauricio Sulano receipting-name flourishing at the bottom.

The moment you spoke to me last night, he told her, I knew you are no ordinary woman. Looking at her bare legs, you're really very attractive, you know. You shouldn't cover yourself up.

Do you really think so? she receiving his gratuities with

pleasure, recalling her mother's unrequited hopes: lie to me, deceive me, but love me; which her father would not ever, he being absolutely honest.

Yes, said Mauricio, I felt you are a very sensitive woman who has been hurt; you've closed yourself off, shut away your heart. Stared through the arnel shift at her heart beneath the lycra brassiere, at the same time tucked the cheque in the shirt pocket over his. Simply said. Come here, Rebecca, to which she responded with the curiosity of a child, the wonder being in the command. Come here. Rebecca, from a man other than her father. He held her to him with measured firmness, not too tight, but close enough. Stroking her back, up and down, resolutely, rhythmically. She softening like a cat. Being led to the couch, which actually was right at the back of the knees, yet she had the feeling of being led: and while she was deciding what, if anything, she was prepared to permit next, depending on his approach to the situation predictable, he took her hands in his, saying,

I must leave now. I have to go to my brother's shop and let him go home to lunch.

Rolling down his sleeves, buttoning one button, then the other, like a storekeeper closing up shop. Putting away the four empty bottles in a beer carton behind the curtain. Replacing the unsold seven canvases carefully, painted side to wall at the head of the couch. Leaving everything nice and tidy. There was in his precise movements an indecent finality. He was leaving. Through the trap door. Carrying out (her) *Stillborn No. 3*. In one hand. Holding out the other (free) hand to help her down (and out). Faceless face of him upturned, assuming deal closed. She felt cheated. Oh it wasn't the money: the picture had plenty of mileage for talk on cold winter nights; it was the fact that she had lost again. Somebody wins, somebody loses. What?

Just a minute, Betty said.

Mauricio halted, apprehensive, indecisive for the first time. Quick fear covering his eyes like a cataract. He needn't be afraid, he had selected carefully if he only knew. She took her defeats with passivity: the children lied to her boldly: Bernie dedicated his book to his mother: the plumber sent his apprentice.

Here, she said, reaching into her purse and holding out a ten-dollar (American) bill, which was her allowance for presents for her children. Here, she said, be a good guy and bring us both some lunch. Urging, take a taxi if you have to, but come back soon, I'm starved. He took the money, clear-eyed again with relief.

Alone. Well, she's supposed to be at the beach, isn't she, might as well get her sunburn while waiting. To be fed? Out on the roof in her bathing suit, weak with a hunger that is not entirely visceral. At her feet a grass mat (I sleep outside and count the stars, he had said). The sun assails the exposed skin; hot trade winds pull at her hair. She lies down on the mat on her back, her head weighted down by a ballast of stale thoughts, she is weary of carrying them about. She jettisons the rotting cargo. Into the empty hold of her mind rush images of black bodies, dying and dead, of slave ships and chains: and black women and black babies, mute as stone; to be joined by burning-eyed skeletons from Belsen; and victims all, black and white, they link arms, slaves and Jew and whirl in a wild *hora* to the trumpeting of "The Birth of the Blues." She sits up. Sweating. Despondent. Yet the sun still shines; the sky is full of pigeons and 'planes. She stands up and walks slowly around the roof: keep moving, she tells herself, like someone lost in the desert, keep moving. All about her is a prairie of flat roofs. Compass-eyes give her her bearings: directly across the narrow street is the empty sun-deck of the Convento (her) Hotel. The absurdity of the juxtaposition: same sun, same air, the only difference being she is here instead of there. Not so terrible. Exploring further, on the other side of the little (tin) shack, she finds a tap and a basin, which she fills and pours the water over her head. It's a shock, but feels good. The cold water dislodges her thoughts and causes her spine to shiver. Again, filling the basin and gasping against the cold, happily alive with discomfort: oh it was just lovely at the beach, yes I had a wonderful time, jumping in the waves (fill and pour), huge waves that high right over my head. Now she is drenched and weary of. Everything.

Lies down again on the mat, face down, with her head beneath her arm, extinguishing the light. Decapitated in the dark universe. Emptied. Weightless. Released, she has the sensation of being space floating off into space. She thinks, how many times does nothing go into nothing and what's left over. She thinks, and becomes a prisoner again. She tries to undo the links of thought but cannot discover how to stop thinking by thinking about not thinking. It's like trying to drown yourself with an approved life-jacket securely harnessed around your shoulders. Ophelia would have gone to the bottom if she had worn a bathing suit instead of all those petticoats and what would old William have done then. Without a corpse, without a body there is not much to write about. Ripeness is all. Oh she is ripe, done to a turn, ready to eat or be eaten, she doesn't care which. She hears. The trap door? Mauricio is back, silent on his sneakers. He brings, oh it is delicious, and cold cokes. How good he tastes, slightly salty, and he is no weight at all and no barrier exists between them. The sun overhead officiates at the *entente cordiale*; the heat seals an ancient bargain. That's how it will be when Mauricio returns. If.

With slow grace, Mauricio stepped backward and Betty followed. She looking around inside and seeing first as she should two walls hung solid with paintings. Fields and flowers; the sea and ships; streets of San Juan.

Did you paint all these pictures?

Do you like them?

No. They're just big postcards.

Then I didn't paint them.

You're putting me on.

What do you mean?

You're fooling me; you did paint them: they have your name on them.

That's only my name: my name doesn't mean a thing; it's my signature that matters. I buy up this stuff by the dozen, I even commission some, the tourists love them. My brother and I are in business; he finds the painters and I make the arrangements; and he sells them, a few at a time. He has five kids, so I let him keep most of the money. I just want enough for paints and a bottle of beer. Would you like a drink of beer?

Sure.

Just one place to sit, an old couch, it had a clean green cover, though. Everything, she noticed, was clean. And tidy. Whitewashed ten-test walls. Fresh starched cotton print curtains closed off one corner. In the middle of the room facing the couch, an empty canvas on an easel. Nearby, on a formica covered table a straight row of paint tubes and clean (new?) brushes. Clean white shirt on a hanger; clean white towel on a rack. Surgical. Would you like some more anaesthetic, he asked. (Actually he said beer.) This won't hurt a bit. (Actually he opened another bottle.) Sitting drinking from bottles on the couch the sag of which threw them together in the middle touching, comfortable and comforting. She asking, he telling, his own work got critical reviews but didn't sell. Mauricio brought out limp folded newspaper clippings from under the pillow (clean white case). Handling them carefully, like a miser. His own work. She asking to see and he carrying canvases to her from corner at head of couch. Where they had been standing hidden, covered by (clean) white sheet.

Eight paintings, his, of concentric circles, of all sizes and colours, filling each canvas one way or another. The eye forced to focus on the cores of the larger circles, whirling like suns, in the exact centre of each, unmistakably, a black, blind embryo. In the lower right hand corner, instead of a name, his signature: a flag, a white field, black bordered, and in the middle, the same black cross seen on the landings.

I call this my Stillborn Series, numbers one to eight. (Deep sigh.) That's my fate, unborn and nameless.

Oh come now, she said, you have a beautiful name and you definitely got yourself born.

You don't understand—no white person really understands.

Try me.

Ah the agony of the closed circle; you die within it; you never emerge into the full light, you never get born.

Now really I've never met anyone more alive than you are this moment. You merely have to learn to *play* dead in the ghetto. Then you go about the business of living; somehow you eat, you love, you begat, you survive.

Easy for you to say: Jews know how to get along better than anybody. I bet your husband has a good job. What does he do?

He's a psychologist; chief consultant for our school system.

You see. Now where would I ever have had the chance to be a psychologist. If I didn't sell lousy pictures to the tourists, I'd have to sweep floors and wash dirty dishes. How do you like my paintings, they're not too expensive.

Betty thinks, you weren't (still) born yesterday; she says, I find them very interesting, the obsessive quality communicates directly.

Mauricio not thinking, just says, I suppose so; anyway I try to express my feelings. The large ones are five hundred; these three hundred. No? You can have this smaller one for a hundred bucks, even.

Inside, she dried off the sweat with his (clean) towel. Dressed. Hungry. Ravenous really. Behind the prim starched curtains finding a small shiny pot and a small shiny kettle on a camp stove. Ah. Two tins of Campbell's tomato soup. Lifting both and almost dropping them in fright, as if scorpions, they, the malevolent pop-art cans being empty of content. But washed clean. A rage in her hands. Chucking the empty tins out on the roof. Spastic hands opening and closing with frustration. Nothing to take hold of. No guns, no knives, not even a can-opener. Oh he knew his victims, just soft brushes and soft soap. He thought. Headed straight for his Stillborns, pulled them out from behind the couch and set them up, one by one, against the wall opposite like clay pigeons. Despite her rage, she stood not without respect before the canvases; art was art, even if only come-ons. She found a tube on the table, a colour called Cadmium Deep Yellow, it never having been opened, well she would do the only honest painting around here. Taking her time, like a true artist, she painted on each of the seven canvases, at the upper left hand, kitty-corner from his black cross. But larger than his insignia—she painted two firm straight overlapping yellow triangles, no wavering now—the Star of David.

Herself through the trap-door, collecting en route *No. 3* where he'd left it resting against the little ladder. Down the stairs. Out into the cool court-yard, no longer reached by the sun. The little girl, now with her mother, laughing on the balcony. Out in the street again, mingling with the other tourists, Betty wishing them better luck with their shopping.

Don't touch me, his wife said, I got badly burned.

At the beach?

At the beach.

You should have known better, first time out in the sun.

I know, but it's so easy to miscalculate. It's always the same: you don't feel it at the time; it's only later that it hurts.

HOLD THAT TIGER

The blue slip inside my envelope directed me, this year, to a converted warehouse on Harbour Street. I hadn't been in Toronto for years and looked forward to seeing old landmarks in the city where I was born. For the occasion I bought a grey suit, a new shirt and tie. All the employees, all 53,969 of us, all over the world, must take the Company's ADAPT exam: Annual Development and Advancement Program Test. The objective of Personnel, we have been assured, is entirely a paternal one, stemming from the Company's interest in each and every one of its workers: It wants to know merely that we are happy in our work and leading productive lives.

I entered a doorway beside a Scandinavian furniture store. I ascended four flights of stairs so narrow I had to let my arms hang lest I bump an elbow. Three men preceded me; a woman was behind me; we were 10 minutes ahead of the hour. I followed the procedures of those in front; she would do the same when I was finished. A handprint on the door caused it to open. We entered singly, allowing the door to click shut each time. In my turn, I stood in the exact centre of a long empty corridor, with a single window at each end. In front of me was a plexiglass box mounted on a beam. I stood before it and spoke my Social Insurance Number, whereupon a card was ejected. It had the same number I had just voiced, together with the letter

M and the number 6. I held the card and looked around for M and 6. I saw a forest of plywood partitions, stained brown, arranged in such a way as to appear as a classical maze. Rats and rewards came instantly to mind. Here and there in the labyrinthine entrances and exits a letter and a number appeared. Great confusion set in as dozens of us searched for our places. By the time I found my letter and number and sat down in my cubicle, I was in a sweat.

The Minotaur in this labyrinth was a large writing pad with yellow sheets, lined. Every page had my Social Insurance Number printed at the top right-hand corner. Instructions were on the cover: Answer the following questions in strict numerical order, starting with Number 1 and ending with Number 10. Refrain from giving false or misleading information: Replies will be verified by Personnel. No partial answers. No equivocation. No talking or consorting with other candidates. A box lunch will be provided at 12:00 hours. A bell will ring for breaks at 10:00 and 14:30 hours. Remember your aisle and seat number. Good luck.

Although the partitions were only about five feet high they were three feet off the floor, so that you could not see over them. Anyone wishing to check on us could peer under the partitions and see pairs of feet at desks. But, of course, that would not be necessary. It came to me that the fire sprinklers, located overhead between the fluorescent lights, were not all vertical: Some were pointed at angles and their ends were closed off with a shiny, black material. These were cameras.

In each cubicle were two desks facing in opposing directions, against the partitions, so that we sat back to back. I was curious to know who shared my part of the maze but did not dare turn around. I dropped my pen. I went down on all fours, pretending to search, and saw a woman's slim legs from under a black skirt, her ankles locked around the chair. She was already writing rapidly, a cheek resting against her left palm.

All 10 questions were printed on the first (unlined) page. Quickly I read them, as I had at school, to test my knowledge against that of my inquisitor. But these questions were unlike any in the past. Their purpose was not clear; there was no logical sequence. A sense of desperation came over me; I would spend the day providing answers for a computer. For some reason, today, I could not bring my mind to address itself again to a machine. I shall imagine that you, young woman scribbling away behind my back, will be the reader of my words. I will talk to you.

*

Question 1: Do you have any obsessions that are likely to interfere with your daily duties?

Answer: There are certain preferences I have that, I suppose, have become obsessive. But since these inclinations, as I prefer to think of them, are part of my daily life outside of my time with the Company, they do not interfere with my work. I do have certain fixed habits: I shave with a strop razor; all my socks are black, even the two pair I wear inside my jogging shoes; I eat my salad last; the top sheet of my bed must be securely tucked in at the foot, tucked in all the way up the far side and halfway up on the near side; I use shirt cardboards for telephone numbers, holding them together with three loose-leaf metal rings. The foregoing are examples of a few routine habits, but since I am not given to unreasonable behaviour, further cataloguing would be of no interest.

On second thought, I do have one obsession—at least everyone has called it that. No one must touch, that is, move in any way, my three toy replicas on my desk.

*

Question 2: Are you afraid of any of the following: Mice. Lice. A man's arm around your shoulder. A woman's screams.

Answer: All of the above. I am terrified of mice and rats. In the places we lived there were always mice and sometimes rats. I hid under the blanket for fear of the rats I heard all night, even in my sleep. I keep my hair cut as short as possible, a crew cut it's called, because of my fear of lice. In Grade 2 I was accused of having brought lice into the classroom. My head was covered with them, the nurse said. I had to have my head shaved. If anything in my life could be deemed to be obsessive, it is the fear of a man's arm about my shoulder. This had to do with a policeman holding me back from running to my mother who was being taken away, screaming.

*

There was the sound of a bell, a lovely, light tone, the kind one hears in a temple. It was the first break. I turned my head to the left, in the direction of the exit from our cell (I have come to think of this cubicle as our cell), pretending to be ruminating on the next question, but hoping to catch a glimpse of my companion. I listened intently. In the silence I could hear the hum of the air conditioner, the occasional cough or clearing of a throat. She sighed a long, drawn-out sigh, but did not go out. Visions of an Ariadne, of a young and beautiful princess, whose perfume even now reached me, who would love me at sight and lead me safely out of the labyrinth—thoughts of an impossible love distracted me from the real business.

*

Question 3: The psychological profile established by Personnel indicates that you have been in the past, and most of the time still are, a steady, intelligent and productive employee; at other times, most markedly since the 1964 Select Employees' Conference in Amsterdam, your profile graphs are erratic. Can you account for the variations in performance?

Answer: In the 15 years I have been with the Company I have tried to be a loyal worker. Above all, I have tried to be honest and truthful. But my work has gone unnoticed. Moreover, I am often called in to elucidate what did I mean by this memo, that letter or some phone call. Soon after my third ADAPT exam I was transferred to the Leamington office. About a year later I became aware that my telephone doodles were being taken out of the wastebasket while I was in the washroom; that my brown paper bag containing my lunch was being opened and the contents examined; a typist from the typists' pool would bring a tape recorder instead of a notebook. The following year I was moved from the front office to a windowless inside room.

At home, our usually convivial evenings were spent in an exchange of monosyllables. My wife and I slept back to back. She sensed that our difficulties were due to my work and began to ask questions. I said very little because I am not in the habit of taking any one into my confidence. This is due, perhaps, to the fact that I have always had to fight my own battles. Just the same she used her considerable intelligence to put together a picture of frustration. She thought I ought to protest such cavalier treatment. I said, "So long as I am being paid by the Company I have no right to object." In reply, she quoted Ambrose Bierce: "Fidelity is a virtue peculiar to those who are about to be betrayed." But to whom should I complain and of what specifically? Then I hit upon a solution, the exercise of which accounts, possibly, for the changes in my graph.

When I was in my early teens, my foster mother used to say, Never lie: A liar becomes a thief, a thief becomes a murderer! Images of being hanged, drawn and quartered;

images of my hands being cut off; images of being seated in a chair with wires to my shaved head; images that made me resolve never to tell a lie.

There are people who believe that Truth, like Time and Space, is relative. I say, tell that to the boy in the orphanage who lines up for adoption, his face aching from the smile he holds. That boy knows Truth Absolute.

Still, to live is to manipulate the truth. For myself, I devised a system of compromise. On Tuesday, Thursday and Saturday I always tell the truth as I see it. Those are the days with the accusatory "u's" in them. On those days I face the memory of my foster mother's troubled eyes. You, they blaze, are lying! At the end of each Tuesday, Thursday or Saturday I feel cleansed. I am at peace. But on Monday, Wednesday and Friday I suspend the truth. I dissemble, hedge, misrepresent, evade, disguise the facts. I sometimes lie outright. Paradoxically, it is often on a Monday, Wednesday or Friday that I am invited out for a drink after work by my superior.

In this manner a balance is struck between conscience and necessity. A flexibility in regard to Truth may appear as instability on my psychological profile.

*

Do you think, young woman in our cell, I have been prolix? But Saturday is Truth Day and I must adhere to some principle, even one of my own invention. Incidentally, just between us, do you not find it reprehensible that this annual exam is held on our, not the Company's, time . . . ?

*

Question 4: Did you report in sick this past year? If so, how long were you absent and what was the nature of your illness?

Answer: On May 22 (it was a Wednesday) I had the apartment super phone the office to say that I had a sore throat and fever and could not come in to work. I took that time off in order to see an old friend. I had read in the newspaper that Frederick Childerhouse would be in Toronto for a few days to negotiate a takeover. I couldn't get through to him on the telephone, even with person-to-person calls. Finally I dialled direct, whatever the cost, and told three secretaries that I was a reporter from *The Globe and Mail* wanting an interview for the front page of the business section. Fred called me back. I heard that hollow echo one gets from one of those phone arrangements where there is no receiver to hold against the ear: One speaks into the air while facing a machine on the desk, and it, the machine, replies into the room. It said, Jack, you old son-of-a-gun, how are you? I could tell he was pleased as punch to hear from me. It invited me to lunch the next day.

I took my time getting ready, choosing a tie carefully. I even went to the bank so that I could face Fred with money in my pocket.

We lunched at the Toronto Club. I liked the hushed atmosphere, the dark, polished wood, the heavy silver, the obsequious service. Fred said he would have known me anywhere. I said he hadn't changed at all, except for a little grey at the temples. His hair was thick, his frame lean. He was as handsome as I remembered him. Just a few thin red veins down the side of his nose were the only signs of the attrition of time.

Mostly we spoke of the decision we had made, solemnly and ceremoniously, to deliberately fail our last year in Jarvis Collegiate. Neither of us knew then how to change our lot in life: his being to go to the university and success; and mine to go to work and uncertainty. That last year of high school Fred played drums in a jazz cellar and I went to hear him. Sometimes I took Rose-Lynn with me. Fred remembered her.

"She liked you. She liked you a lot. I thought for sure you two would wind up getting married," he recalled.

"Rose-Lynn was sent away to school in Switzerland at the end of our last year at Jarvis," I told him. "I never saw her again."

"In those days . . . " he began, then fell silent. After a while he said, "I haven't picked up a pair of sticks since I graduated."

By three in the afternoon he was telling me about his two marriages, the two divorces and how he manages to keep in touch with each of his eight children.

In my turn, I told him about Vivian; that like myself she felt alone in the world; that we got married three months after we met at the Adult Resources Centre.

"She died in childbirth, eight years ago," I said simply.

Our visit ended with pleasantries but with no reference to the future.

As to the "nature of your illness" . . . I suppose it could be termed a kind of sickness, this persistent illusion that somehow I would be transformed from a clerk in Leamington, riding on the Number 18 bus daily, into one of Fred's vice-presidents flying on the Concorde.

*

Question 5: Upon hearing a dance beat that goes: *tee*-dum-dum, *tee*-dum-dum, *tee*-dum-dum, *tee*-dum-dum; and upon receiving instructions and diagrams that indicate dance steps, *one*-two-back, *one*-two-side, *one*-two-back, *one*-two-side—would you:

(a) Do the fox trot or the cha-cha?

(b) We have in our files a photograph of you holding a dance trophy and shaking hands with Trump Davidson at the Palace Pier in 1948. Explain.

Answer: (a) I no longer dance.

(b) Through Fred I became interested in, then addicted to, jazz. I discovered I could dance as naturally as I could breathe. Every Saturday night, Rose-Lynn and I went dancing at the Palace Pier. She was slight, blonde and, like me, lived to dance. I was 18, she was 16. So well-matched were we that other dancers would stop to watch us. Our favourite dance, which became our contest number, was *Tiger Rag*. And when the trombone repeated *Hold That Tiger!* over and over, we charged down the length of the dance floor, returned to the bandstand in a variety of steps, and charged down again to the other end. Life could offer no more: I had a job and a beautiful dance partner; I won prizes.

*

Ah, my unknown love, I feel your concentration, your rigid spine behind me. Are you wondering, at this very instant, who cares about your replies? In all these years I have never discovered what happens to my print-outs. There has been no sign, ever, that I have made an impression on anyone. The man who, possibly, holds my future in his hands is someone not unlike myself, with a fresh haircut, clean shirt and a discreet tie. He reads with understanding and sympathy, as he recalls his own exam that took place recently or will take place soon. In my imagination he makes some sort of entry on my dossier, then passes it on, together with this print-out, to the next authority. It is my hope, dear colleague, that you fare better than I. Take your time; don't fret; do not attempt to influence the results: We reveal ourselves no matter what we say.

*

Question 6: Describe a community activity in which you have participated, the nature of your contribution and outline the relevance it had for you.
Answer: When I was 20 I lived in a rooming house on Clinton Street. There I was befriended by an older man, Wilhelm Schroeder. He was an idealist. He believed that the working class would one day own the means of production. He was editor and printer of a Marxist newspaper called *The New Proletarian*. Bill, as I called him, urged me

to give up my job with the capitalist exploiter manufacturer. (His words.) That didn't take much persuasion because I worked in the factory basement as a shipper. For a while I was out of work, but Bill shared everything he had with me. We were like father and son. He gave me a present of his most precious possession, all that he had left of his childhood: toy miniatures of Hitler, Goering and Goebbels. Naturally I was startled at first—the verisimilitude was frightening. Bill noted my hesitation. He said that they were after all only toys; that he had spent many happy hours playing with them. I promised I would never part with them. You must understand that these replicas were the first gifts I had ever received. I see now that it is very important to face things that one is afraid of in order to conquer fear. But I digress.

I helped Bill set type. I also delivered copies of the paper. My territory was bounded by Bathurst and Dufferin, Bloor and King streets. Once a week I was stationed on the corner of Queen and Spadina handing out leaflets. This community activity ended when Bill left for Montreal because his typewriter, filing cabinet and printing machine were smashed with axes by vandals one night. He claimed it was the work of communists.

For me, the relevance of this social activity was that I gave hope and inspiration to the poor and the dispossessed.

*

Question 7: If you were a Company scout and had to stake out the Hotel Krasnapolsky in Amsterdam, would you disguise yourself as:

    (a) a waiter

      a salesman of Perrier

      a reporter covering the meeting of the Club of Rome

      other

    (b) Why?

*

This was going to take some thought. My fingers were cramped; I pulled them one by one. While I was deliberating on giving an honest answer to imagining myself as someone else, I became aware that a cart had stopped in the aisle beside us. I wondered if she knew the procedure for obtaining lunch. I stood up and tapped her on the shoulder. She turned, and I took advantage of the next moment to look into her face. She had a small nose and mouth and a broad forehead; large dark eyes and straight brows that almost met and which gave her a worried look. She smiled at me. I pointed to the sign on the robot: FOR LUNCH RAISE RIGHT HAND IN FRONT OF ELECTRONIC EYE MARKED "E". She did. The ticking sound was replaced by a whirring noise. She watched in fascination as a box lunch was deposited at the corner of her desk. Then it was my turn, and the arm released a box from its claw onto my desk.

I ate out of the cardboard box. A baloney sandwich on white bread; yellow mustard on the side; tiny yellow biscuits in the shape of fish and marked Goldfish, two to a package and two packages in the lunch; a piece of yellow cheese marked Colby and a white paper napkin. All were individually sealed in plastic. There was a can of pop called Fresh Up. I nibbled and considered. The question may have something to do with the 1964 meeting in Amsterdam. I was one of the specially chosen employees from the Company's worldwide plants and subsidiaries. Had we been infiltrated by an industrial spy? By the CIA? By the RCMP? Was I supposed to know something . . . ?

*

Answer: (a) I would disguise myself as a reporter for a chain of American newspapers and cover the meetings of the Club of Rome.

(b) Since I am experienced in the field of newspaper publication, I feel I would succeed in the guise of a reporter. I could have been a writer, everyone said so at school. At any rate, I have always read a great deal and am well-informed and could ask the correct questions. And since the Club of Rome produces large-scale computer studies, resulting in massive amounts of data, I am certain I could elicit information useful to the Company.

*

Question 8: Point out, briefly, which aspects of the Select Employees' Conference in 1964 you found to be most valuable to your career.

Answer: The second day's presentations and subsequent discussions on *Interdependence* were most illuminating. I realized then that each and every one of us in the Company performs a function vital to someone else. Without my input, another person cannot do his or her job.

*

They know. I thought I was off the hook; no one ever said anything to me about that last day. Now I see that they have just been biding their time . . .

Ariadne, my love, are you at this very moment complying with simple requests that you tell them who your favourite movie stars are? What suggestions you have for the improvement of the food in the cafeteria? Perhaps you have hopes, illusions, desires. You think your answers will bring a recognition of your great potential. Beware. You are being lulled into a feeling that all is well at the palace. In time, should you work for the Company long enough, you will be asked questions that force you to dredge up the mold and miasma from the dungeons. The computer is not only your confessor, but also judge-executioner.

The bell sounds. You raise your head. Your chair scrapes. I see you leave. You walk briskly.

*

Question 9: When your wife stood in the doorway to the living room where you were sitting with the newspaper, and she stood there, half-turned to come into the room or

half-turned to leave, and asked, Do you love me?—what
was your reply?
Answer: In my heedless youth, the question angered me.
Perhaps because it confused me. I thought that everything
pointed to my love for Vivian. I worked. I saved. I was faith-
ful. I came home every night, ate, unbuckled and slept. On
Monday, Wednesday and Friday, I said, Of course I love
you, my darling. On Tuesday, Thursday or Saturday, I had
to tell her, I don't know what love is; perhaps it is only a
chemical charge for the propagation of the species.

*

Ah, my Ariadne, you're back, your hair combed, lipstick
renewed. You dare not look at me, you lower your eyes,
you bump against your chair. As for me, I am not afraid
to stare at you openly and frankly. I may even speak to
you when we are finished. Nothing I do from now on will
make any difference. The die is cast; my fate is sealed.

*

Question 10: Why are there no asides or soliloquies in
Ibsen's play *Ghosts*?
Answer: Because the facts speak for themselves. The sins of
the fathers. Sin. An illicit pleasure—once only—and the
drama unfolds, inexorably, inevitably. No chorus of com-
ments is necessary.

It was the last night of the 1964 Select Employees' Conference in Amsterdam. At dinner I sat beside Sam Milner
of our Windsor plant. Just before the coffee and the final
lecture, we slipped outside for a breath of air.

We found ourselves on an old narrow street behind the
hotel. We kept walking, stopping now and again to examine
with fatal curiosity the displays in the "Love Shops." We
also stopped in front of old houses, high and narrow, in
whose ground-floor windows sat smiling women, beckon-
ing. In one window, built over the street, sat a young blonde
woman, knitting under a lamp, a ball of blue wool secured

between her thighs. She looked like any housewife, resting on a chair with lace doilies, behind a sparkling window with starched curtains.

And while we strolled and gaped and poked one another and made lewd remarks like schoolboys, Vivian, a thousand miles away, alone in our house, went unexpectedly into labour. A mother fell at a bus stop and broke her wrist and did not reach her daughter in time.

Sam and I dared each other. It was the first time either of us had been in Europe. We went back down the street and bought prophylactics. And while the other 198 specially selected employees were sitting in the Hotel Krasnapolsky, being hectored on marketing methods, we entered the houses.

And while I was paying a stranger for the act of love, Vivian's dark head was tossing in agony. While I was exhausting myself on that compliant woman, the lifeblood of my wife was ebbing away. Vivian died. The baby died.

Back home, I picked up our wedding picture, my three toy figures and a few books and left everything behind.

*

Do you, Ariadne, hold the thread that will save me? The monster still stalks this labyrinth; he will not be slain. He is Memory.

WHAT HAPPENED TO RAVEL'S BOLERO?

Sylvia sipped her martini from the plastic bathroom tumbler, not taking her eyes off the light patches of paint on the wall opposite. Her teeth chattered; she put the tumbler down on the bare floor. Richard said, "They haven't put the heat on yet." He poured himself another martini from the glass jar into a paper cup he held in his other hand. Some of the liquid spilled down the side of the jar, onto his bare thigh. Sylvia leaned over and licked his skin. He laughed like a boy and spilled a bit more. They were undressed and sat close together at the far end of the sofa. She picked up her drink. "Are you going back to your wife?" she asked. He lifted the glass jar and held it in the air and said, "Cheers." This time he gulped from the bottle. He began to undress her the moment she came through the door: he could never wait. She kicked off her shoes. On the wall opposite were two square patches of light gray paint. "The pictures, the ones I gave you?" she asked. "My sons came up in the station wagon over the week-end and took everything they could carry." Sylvia sipped from the tumbler. Her teeth chattered. He put his robe around her shoulders.

Richard lay stretched out the full length of the sofa, his long white legs muscular for his age. On the wall opposite over the table where they often ate there were two square patches of light gray paint. She got on top of him. "Are you going to sleep with your wife?" Sylvia wanted to know. In the darkening room she could not make out his expression. When she sat up the juices drained out of her on the cloth; even now she had to look closely to see an unevenness of colour in the middle cushion. He stood up and she put her face into the soft flesh of his belly; she smelled their sweat on his skin. Sylvia thought her purse felt heavier with the weight of the articles she had taken. She smiled up at him. Together they got up and started towards the bedroom.

Sylvia sipped from the plastic tumbler. The rugs were rolled up, her clothes were all over the bare floor, one shoe near the window, her dress in a heap. The rough brown cloth would absorb his ejaculation which dripped out of her when she sat up. Richard was wearing the wool tartan bathrobe she had given him that first Christmas. She had never seen him in house slippers. "What's wrong?" she asked immediately. "I think I'm catching a cold," Richard said. She could not find her other shoe. Her teeth chattered; she put the tumbler down on the bare floor. He gulped from the bottle. This time when she came in, having let herself into the apartment with a key she kept separate in a red leather case, she had to seek him out. He was in the kitchen; in front of him on the counter were a bottle of gin and a bottle of vermouth. He was wearing the bathrobe she had given him that first Christmas. He couldn't find anything to mix the martinis in; he opened and banged shut the cupboard doors. The cupboards were empty. The first desperate clutching, followed by sticky stuff seeping out of her all over the middle cushion when she sat up, but the rough brown synthetic material dried quickly. She stared at the empty hi-fi cabinet. "What's wrong?" Sylvia asked when she found him in the kitchen. "I've been asleep," Richard said, "I took the day off; I don't feel well." His wife will have the sofa cleaned, Sylvia thought. He was pale and kept his face averted. "The movers are coming in the morning," Richard said. He could never wait to make love to her. She put the palm of her hand against his forehead: it was hot. She got down on all fours and searched for the other shoe under the sofa. He looked at her finally and then away again. He couldn't find what he wanted in the empty cupboards and banged each door shut. Sylvia watched him consider an almost empty olive jar. He dumped a half dozen olives on the counter. She brought out the ice cubes. "What's wrong?" Sylvia kept asking. "I've been transferred to New York. I'll be working out of Head Office." (His familiar bony face with the deep line down each cheek.) When he saw that she was not going to make a scene, he turned to face her. His brown eyes were clouded over. Side by side on the sofa, undressed, they drank martinis. He could never wait to make love to her. Across the room, against the wall opposite, at the oak table where they used to eat, she observed there was one chair and one place setting on the table in front of the chair. While he was under the shower she started to pick up her clothes. She couldn't find the other shoe.

Richard gulped the martini straight from the glass jar. "Does your wife still love you?" Sylvia asked. He moved to the end of the sofa, farthest from her, because the middle cushion was wet. (But the rough brown cloth would absorb the moisture.) Her teeth chattered; she put down the empty tumbler on the bare floor. He looked at her and away again. Together they got up and started towards the bedroom. She stopped at the corner to the little hall to look at the empty hi-fi cabinet. The second time, in his bed, was to be for her satisfaction. On top of the dresser were his wrist watch, wallet, keys and a Texaco bill. The dresser drawers were empty. He got under the covers, his feet were cold, as were hers, the heat had not come on yet in the apartment even though it was the middle of October. Together they got up and started towards the bedroom. She stopped to look at the hi-fi cabinet. The shelves were empty, the record compartments were empty. "What happened to Ravel's *Bolero*?" Sylvia asked. "Darling, I'm sorry, but my sons cleared out everything they could carry. I didn't dare say anything," Richard said. She turned and went first into the bathroom. She stretched out in the bed. She watched him go into the bathroom. When he returned she arched her back while he placed a towel under her. The second time, in the bed, where they could move more freely, was to be for her satisfaction. On top of the dresser were his wrist watch, wallet, keys and a Texaco bill. She picked up the bill and asked, "Is this where you live on Long Island?" He snatched the paper out of her hand.

Sylvia waited until he came out of the bathroom. "Will I see you again?" she asked. "We had to come to the end of the road some time. This is it," Richard told her. Over the dresser where the mirror used to hang was an oblong patch of light gray paint in contrast with the darker paint. Richard snatched the bill out of her hand. She watched him go into the bathroom. Blowing his nose and shuffling in his slippers Richard looked old. The bedroom was at the back of the building and was quiet, unlike the living room which echoed the constant noise of traffic on Avenue Road. She lay down on the towel. The second time was to be for her pleasure. "How old is your wife?" Sylvia asked. "Same age as I am," Richard replied. He pulled the towel from under her and wiped his groin. All the same, their love-making was not entirely successful. She began to dress, picking up her garments one by one from the bare floor. He lay with his eyes shut. The dresser drawers were empty. She arched her back while he placed a towel under her. "Do you have

twin beds or a double bed in your house on Long Island?"
Sylvia wanted to know. In reply Richard said, "She is not
like you in bed: she hasn't your energy." The elevators were
still, everyone having gone out or decided to stay in for the
evening. She had not been satisfied. His feet were cold, but
his face when he kissed her was hot. He snatched the bill
out of her hand. "It's a big promotion," he said later, "vice-
president in charge of personnel. 82,000 employees, all over
the world. I will have to live up to the job." He had small
teeth that didn't suit his large features. She watched him
go into the bathroom. On the oak table where they used
to eat was a place setting for one. She couldn't find her other
shoe. The dresser drawers were empty.

Sylvia pulled the drapes in the living room and lit the
lamps. The sofa cushions were reversible. She began to pick
up her clothes. On the oak table was set out a plate, a linen
napkin in a sterling silver ring, a knife, fork and spoon, and
sterling silver salt and pepper shakers. They went towards
the bedroom. Where the mirror had hung opposite the bed
there was an oblong patch of light gray paint on the wall.
She would wait to comb her hair when he came out of the
shower. "My sons took the records." She knew he referred
to Ravel's *Bolero* which she had bought him for his birthday. Yet their love-making was not entirely successful. The
dresser drawers were empty. "Where are my things?"
Sylvia asked. "Darling, I'm sorry. The incinerator. I had no
choice." His wrist watch, wallet and keys were on top of
the dresser. She picked up the Texaco bill with his name
and address imprinted in carbon from a credit card. "Is this
where you live on Long Island?" she asked. Richard
snatched the paper out of her hand; he put it in his wallet
in front of the bills. He put the watch on his wrist and the
keys in his pocket.

Sylvia let herself into the apartment with a key she kept
separate in a red leather case. At first she thought he was

out. Then she found him in the kitchen, looking for something in the cupboards. She saw the cupboards were empty. When she came in, he pulled his bathrobe together over his bare chest, tightening the sash. He looked at her then away again. "What's wrong?" Sylvia asked. He kept his face averted. "The movers are coming in the morning," Richard replied. She brought out the ice cubes. He gulped from the bottle. "Cheers," he said, holding up the glass jar. When he saw that she was not going to make a scene he turned towards her. "I think I'm catching a cold," he said. His brown eyes were clouded over. They moved more freely in the bed. Before she went into the bathroom, she covered him with a blanket. The first thing his wife will do will be to have the sofa cleaned, Sylvia reflected. She noticed her purse where she had left it on the oak table where they sometimes ate. When he saw she was not going to make a scene, Richard began to undress her; he couldn't wait to make love to her. Some of the liquid spilled down the side of the jar onto his bare thigh. Sylvia bent over and licked his skin. He laughed like a boy. He snatched the bill out of her hand. Blowing his nose and shuffling in his slippers Richard looked old. She kicked off her shoes and one landed hear the windows. "Listen," Richard said, "if you ever get to New York . . . "

He took off his robe and put it around her shoulders. Her teeth chattered. When she sat up the juices drained out of her onto the middle cushion, but the rough brown cloth absorbed the spill. His narrow white body was in sharp contrast with the dark cloth; she would forever remember the shape of him, she thought to herself. The bedroom was at the back of the building and was quiet. It faced the little gardens of the new condominiums on Oriole Road. She lay down on the towel and pulled the sheet up to her chin. He was apologetic. "My wife told my sons to start moving me back home. They left me with one towel." He never waited:

he began to undress her the moment she came into the apartment. Their love-making was not entirely successful. He pulled the towel from under her and wiped his groin. "Hungry?" Richard asked. "We'll have to go out to eat. Let's go down to Pierre's. You'd like that, eh?" She began to dress. The evening traffic sounded loud in the living room. She went and stood outside the bathroom door to make sure he was still under the shower. She noticed her purse where she had left it on the oak table and picked up the sterling silver napkin ring and the sterling silver salt and pepper shakers and put them in her purse. She snapped the clasp shut. She went down on all fours to look for her other shoe under the sofa. When he strode back into the living room he was fully dressed. He looked distinguished in his dark blue suit, white shirt and dark blue tie with small flecks of red in it. His brown eyes were clear. "You must be hungry," he said, pulling on his cuffs, "we'll go down to Pierre's. You'd like that, Sylvia, eh?" She thought her purse felt heavier with the weight of the silver.

Sylvia remembered she hadn't combed her hair. When he came out of the shower she went into the bathroom and locked the door. She watched him go into the bathroom, admiring his long, lean back and small waist. He came back with a towel. "Does your wife still love you?" He stroked her legs and kissed her breasts. He held her and said, "I have no choice. They're a very conservative company; a family firm run by family men. No private telephones." She began to dress. She got down on all fours to look for her shoe under the sofa. The evening traffic was loud in the living room. She stood outside the bathroom door to make sure he was still under the shower. She snapped the clasp shut. He held the door open. "Will you write?" she asked. "No promises," he replied, stepping backwards. "You're safe with me," she said. "No promises," he repeated. Blowing his nose and shuffling in his slippers he looked old. He held the door open for her. He was distinguished in his dark blue suit. The smell of his shaving cream and cologne was familiar. Sylvia was abstracted and silent. She shifted her purse to her other hand. Now that he knew she would not make a scene he smiled down at her.

THE HOMECOMING

My homecoming was intended to be a surprise. I told them, "There is no point in dragging my husband all the way to Guelph when it is a simple matter for me to get on a train to Toronto." For some reason people are released from institutions on Sunday, perhaps that is the day when someone is free to take the patient home. The full impact of it being Sunday came when I got out of the Union Station. Sunday fills me with despair. It is on Sunday that husband and wife and children spend the day together. They go to church or to other homes or go for a walk, the youngest daughter walking beside her father. And when they are old, husband and wife take a promenade on a sunny Sunday afternoon, his arm in hers. They rest in a café and order rich cakes. Sunday is a family day for families other than mine. In my house, the children and I revolve aimlessly around one another. Doors slam, radios blast, the tv is turned on but nobody watches it. Today, my husband left at dawn for Sunnydale Farms, where his mare is stabled. He will spend the day riding. By this time I was not at all certain how my unannounced return would be received. Instead of going into the subway I followed the signs to the Royal York Hotel and checked in. I sat in my room until it became dark, which, at this time of year, in mid-November, was about five-thirty. I thought, if I come home at dinner-time, I can keep busy until Zbigniew and the children get used to my being in the house again.

The front door was locked. My hands groping inside my purse for the familiar feel of the leather case with its five keys (two car, one back door, one front door and one bank deposit box) came up empty. At the bottom of the bag was only my hotel key on its oversize hardboard tag. I could not remember what I had done with my keys. Had they been taken from me? It took control not to beat upon the door with my fists. Then, by going into the alley between my house and the next, I was able to open the gate to the garden and step up on a cedar deck. Glass doors from the family room open up on the deck, and a careful check proved these to be unlocked. However, I remained standing outside, on the deck, in the dark, in order to observe my husband as he slept in his easy chair.

Zbigniew's face in repose is the face of an aristocrat whose ancestors were in the history books of Poland. I have been shown their pictures; they are, like their displaced descendant, men with blond hair, square faces and small nostrils. Behind his closed lids are blue eyes, imperious in their gaze, which, now that I think of it, never change their colour or expression. Relaxed, his mouth is full and curved; yet I remember it as a mouth with lips that barely open to speak. He will wake precisely at 6:15. Awake or asleep he dreams, I know, of riding his white stallion across his (no longer his) fields, hunched over the sweating back, straining towards a curve in the sky, which he reaches quickly, but he does not stop, because even in that short time the sky has straightened and he sees another curve towards which he must, he absolutely must, with every ounce of strength, reach. I could see him astride the horse in his grandfather's Cossack costume, his knees dug into the stallion's flanks, his bare head against the wind, his coat-tails flying. And should some barrier suddenly loom up between him and that distant ellipse, he and his mount, the two now transformed into a centaur, will transcend the obstacle in a perfect arc. Such were the pictures evoked for me by my husband in the flowery speech of his youth, which, even in translation, I once found poetic. He stirs and reaches for the newspaper that has fallen to the floor at his side. He reads now, unfolding the paper, page by page. Something suddenly causes him to sit upright, draw in a sharp breath, open his mouth in what must be a shout. A woman comes hurrying in, wiping her hands on a towel. The woman's back is to me; and since Zbigniew is absorbed in what he is reading to her he does not see me pull aside one of the glass doors.

That is me he is reading about.

" . . . and she took a taxi to Emergency, wearing a rain-coat over her nightgown, her hair uncombed, in her son's slippers, clutching a large black purse. At the hospital she could only make low moans in reply to routine questions. All the tests, blood and neurological, gynecological exami-nation, a brain scan, X-rays in three dimensions, revealed no pathological cause for her distress. She claimed to have neither husband, children nor other family; nor did she know a doctor. A social worker, by examining the contents of her purse, established that she has a husband and two children and a father. Moreover, in the immediate vicinity there is a private medical clinic, where, it was ascertained, there are records of her, as well as the family. Accompanied by one of the hospital's volunteers (name withheld on re-quest), Mrs. Borowski was returned to her home, where, she kept insisting, she no longer lives."

There is a moment, as after the eulogy at a funeral, when the words are allowed their full impact, to be weighed against the facts. Zbigniew let the newspaper fall; he and the woman were silent. Then he said, "I saw no reason for a private room. She received the same care and the same treatment in the public ward. The practice of medicine does not alter with the price of the bed." There was for me a certain satisfaction that the newspaper report had some impact on him. Moreover, when they left the family room, the woman went ahead and Zbigniew followed with a step that resembled a shuffle. The evidence of his discomfiture gave me the courage to leave the garden and go around to the front door and ring the bell. I was moved also by a desire to see the faces of my two children. This feeling was immediately followed by resentment that *that* woman would be summoning *my* children; in turn, followed by the thought that I could, legally, oust her if I wanted to.

The same woman opened the door.

"Oh, it's you! I've been expecting you!"

She welcomed me, I felt, by the way she held the door open wide, and swung her free arm in a manner that ushered me inside. Perhaps she recognized me from the family snapshots in an album at the bottom of the buffet drawer, under the tablecloths. I stepped into the light.

"I knew you'd turn up sooner or later," she said in an affable voice. She was taller than I and much thinner, so that my black jersey dress was held up only by bony shoulders and pulled together at her waist by a man's brown leather belt. "My name is Francesca," she said.

I could hear water running through the pipes. The children washing up for dinner. I looked at my watch. It was 6:20. Francesca also looked at her watch. "They won't come down until the very last second," she said. "I know, they hate sitting down to dinner with their parents," I said. "Ten minutes," she said. We knew the reference was to Zbigniew who, at this moment, would be in the basement, polishing his riding boots. A tacit understanding arose between Francesca and me; we became bound by identical experiences. "Please stay," she said, "the children will be happy to see you." I handed her my coat which she hung up in the hall closet. "I think they miss you, but I also think they have accepted me. Their lives are not changed."

Anton and Dina came down the stairs together, precisely at 5:30, and said, "Hi Mom," in passing; Zbigniew came through the kitchen at the same time and did not notice me until we were all in the dining room. There was some hesitation where I was to sit, until Zbigniew rose and brought in a chair and placed it to his right. On my right was Dina, Anton across the table and Francesca at my former place at the end nearest the kitchen.

"How have you been?" my husband asked.

"Never better," I smiled at him, "how have *you* been?"

"I've had a bad cold; it hung on for weeks."

Francesca, passing plates of cabbage rolls, said, "I gave him a hot whisky at night and aspirins."

"That was the correct thing to do," I commented. "Are you over your cold?"

"My routine suffered. I'm back on course now."

"Your children," Francesca addressed me, "your children do not like cabbage."

Anton and Dina were suppressing laughter or rage, I could not tell. They made no noise, waiting, I knew, for the ordeal of the dinner hour to be over. Upstairs, under mattresses, was a cache of potato chips and chocolate bars. Their faces vacant, their eyes distrustful—what will become of them, I wondered.

Francesca brought in cookies and peaches for dessert. I had baked the cookies and put them in the freezer; I had canned the peaches on a hot, humid day in September. It crossed my mind that it was too soon to open the canned peaches: they were meant to be served in mid-winter, when their taste would bring memories of summer. I thought, I do not mind you replacing me; I do not mind you feeding my children; but you have no right to take as yours the peaches I sweated over. My anger, habitually, is wordless. Yet, the children always sense what my thoughts are; and I always know by their behaviour how they feel, because they, unlike me, have the capacity or the innocence to act out their discomfort. Anton and Dina rose from the table as if by signal, deliberately scraping their chairs (what happened to the rug?), backing away in mock disgust at the sight of the peaches. Zbigniew laughed. And while they know it is his way of staying out of the situation, they pretend to agree that the situation was funny. In high spirits they ran from the room. The meal ended in the silence I remembered so well. A despised task, the washing up, was welcomed as an escape. I offered to do the dishes. Francesca demurred, saying I was a guest, after all, it was her duty, she didn't mind, it was a privilege for her, and similar protests. The old pull persisted, however, and I picked up four-five dishes to make my exit plausible. Alright, but I was only to rinse and stack: she had her own system for the dishwasher. In the kitchen, each time I turned off the tap, I could hear Francesca's voice in a light, gossipy tone telling Zbigniew something. When she ended her account, there was silence again, until she began another diversion. Against the silences I found relief in the familiar things around me: the patterns of the wallpaper, the patterns of the floor tiles, the patterns of the china. My hands and feet went about their kitchen business without thought on my part. There were even a few moments of pleasure as I put away knives, pots, towel, apron and broom, exactly where they were supposed to go. I worked quietly. My curiosity was aroused: he allows her to chatter, as he did me, without comment; but when he ultimately speaks, as he does just once before he goes back to his newspaper, will he reveal anything new? What he tells her I have heard a thousand times.

"My first horse was thoroughbred Arab stallion, that my grandfather had brought from Hungary on my twelfth birthday. I named him Furioso, which was also the name of his breed. They were well named, those proud, beautiful animals. He was high-tailed, white, with a silky white mane. I kept his coat so shiny it shone even at night. He had wide, dark eyes, neat ears and flared nostrils. O, but he was spirited! No one could come near him, let alone ride him. Even my grandfather, a former Cossack and cavalry officer, was afraid of him. My grandfather intended to beat him into submission, but I asked for a chance to tame him. It was agreed: if I could not ride Furioso within one week, he would be turned into a work horse. I had one of our servants lock me in the stall with the horse. In the morning, at the first light of day, the same terrified servant opened the lock, certain he would find me trampled to death. Instead, I walked out, leading Furioso, who was as submissive as a donkey. I was his master. On two occasions I raced him in Warsaw. We won. How did I subdue him? That will remain my secret forever."

"My guess is it was a matter of superior malice," Francesca said.

Her remark must have puzzled him as it did me: I couldn't decide whether it was intended as praise or as sarcasm. At any rate, it ended Zbigniew's monologue and he went back into the family room. Or perhaps, simply, he glanced at his watch and decided table talk was finished. There was nothing left for me to do, so that when Francesca came in we sat down on stools at the kitchen counter, facing one another.

She said, – Your summer things have been packed in marked cartons. I put white shoe polish on your sandals; they'll be ready to wear the first hot day next summer.

I said, – Those long hot days. Those long hot useless week-ends.

She said, – Zbigniew is pleased that I learned to prepare Polish dishes. I can cook cabbage in many different ways—cabbage rolls, hot cabbage soup with meat or cold cabbage soup with sour cream, coleslaw. There's a crock of cabbage in the basement for sauerkraut.

I said,   – Those long hot nights. I woke in the middle of the night and went out to lie down on the deck in the garden. He didn't wake up. He didn't miss me.

– I have registered for a course in French cooking. I think Zbigniew will like French cooking, the Poles and the French get along well: the French loved Chopin. Zbigniew reads Baudelaire in the original. Did you know your husband wrote a book of poems in French, *The Fields No More*?

– In September I drove to High Park every day. I left the car near the Bloor Street entrance and walked deep into the park. There were lovers everywhere. On the slopes in the sun, behind bushes, on top of picnic tables. They looked as if they might be foreigners. Don't misunderstand me, I mean only that, possibly where they come from there is not that freedom to hug and kiss in the open. Perhaps there were some Canadian lovers also. I couldn't tell. I always took a book with me and held it open in front of me so that they wouldn't catch me staring.

– Zbigniew is so clever, he speaks eight languages and several Slavic dialects. I asked him to help me with my French, but I don't think he has the patience to deal in two languages at night when he must do that all day as a translator in the courts. He didn't say he wouldn't help me; he just didn't.

- In October the light was bright, the air was dry and sharp, leaves crunched underfoot. The lovers didn't see me; they never took their eyes off one another.
- Last Thursday, Zbigniew had a particular trying day. I read about it in the paper. The defendant was from Yugoslavia, his wife Italian and the witness, their landlady, was Portuguese. The husband was accused of keeping his wife tied to a chair, her mouth gagged, while he was at work. The landlady discovered her when she knocked on the door to borrow a cup of oil. The magistrate looked down at the wife who was seated before him, on her chair, still bound and gagged. 'Why didn't the landlady untie her?' he asked. The translator— that's Zbigniew!—said, 'Your honour, she says it is dangerous to interfere in the affairs of married couples. She thinks he must have had good reason for what he did to his wife.' 'Find out,' the judge instructed Zbigniew, 'why he did it.' 'Your honour, he says he did it for her safety. He says she comes from Genoa and goes wandering down around Toronto Harbour and talking to sailors like in the old country.'
- One Sunday morning I went to the park but I didn't stay very long. It was November, the trees were bare, dry leaves whirled and sailed in the wind. The lovers seemed obsessed. In their faces, in the way they clutched each other, was a desperation that one associates with the classic tragedies of star-crossed lovers. There were not many people: we all seemed resigned to something: the old men to walking their

dogs, the dogs resigned to the pace of the old men; the lovers to being satisfied with just a glimpse of the other's face and a touch of the hands; and I to my solitary walk. When it began to rain I took the street car at the Howard Park entrance. I did not go directly home. I walked on Yonge Street, north, on the east side, a walk I had often taken when I was young and idle and lonely. There was a cold drizzle; there were few pedestrians. Before I knew it, it was nine o'clock. I was cold, wet and tired, yet I did not want to go home. The marquee at the New Yorker Cinema was lit up, with *Children of Paradise* in large letters. I went in.

– That same night after dinner Zbigniew and I were alone in the living room. I asked him how the case had ended. He said it had been such a terrible ordeal for him—instructions from the magistrate, the principals all talking at once, the wife when released screaming obscenities in Italian which he had found difficult to translate—that he asked to be taken off the case.

– I stayed to see the film twice. I had to see again that part near the end when Garance and Baptiste embrace and she says to him, 'I never forgot you. You have helped me to live through all these years.' And Baptiste replies, 'I've thought of you every day.' Garance whispers, 'My life was so empty, and I felt so alone. But I told myself, You have no right to be sad, you are one of the happy ones in spite of everything, because someone really loved you.'

– Zbigniew told me that his grandfather had known how to deal with wayward horses— and wayward women. Then, he took the riding crop off its hook at the side of the mantel and struck his palm with it, then thrashed the air around him.

- I came home after midnight. The lights were on in the living room. I glanced in before I hung up my coat in the hall closet. Zbigniew was standing beside the fireplace, his hands behind his back. He followed me up the stairs to the bedroom. In his hand was his grandfather's riding crop, which always hangs on a hook beside the mantel. He didn't say a word. He raised the riding crop. I bent my head, protecting myself with my arms.
- The riding crop belonged to his grandfather, it is only a memento. Zbigniew never uses it, not even on his horse. He put it back on the hook.
- I was afraid. At the same time, I was aware of a contradiction: Zbigniew had often told me he would never whip a horse. I believed him. I have never seen him lose his temper. I used to wonder what would happen if we fought: I would scream accusations at him; perhaps he would hit me; with his hand. I could understand that. I straightened up; I faced him.
- It was only Thursday night, but even so I suggested it would do him good to relax in bed, make love and get a good sleep. He would not make an exception; he kept to his week-day routine and went to sleep after the ten o'clock news.
- He wouldn't look at me. He struck me three times. I felt the whip on my face, my breasts and my legs. He said nothing. We went to bed as usual. We had intercourse as usual.

She said, – I didn't mind. His refusal was not directed against me. He is an honourable man—he has never taken the scissors to my credit cards, as I've heard other husbands do. I am satisfied. It is a good life, this, to live with a virtuous man.

I said, – Virtue is not capacity. To you, however, I offer gratitude, if you require it. Tell me, how soon after I was gone did you move in?

She said, – You left the door unlocked. I was here when Zbigniew came home.

I said, – Then, despite everything, he has been able maintain his schedule?

She said, – To the minute.

Again, the household sounds held me. Overhead were the children's quick steps, a door shut, then another. Francesca and I were both alerted by these sounds; we turned our heads to look at the clock on the wall. A sense of communion jumped between us, so that in a manner of speaking we became one mind. A nod, a look, and wordlessly we confirmed it was 9:30 Sunday night. The anticipated click of the bathroom lock. Zbigniew taking his bath. His instructions, apparently have been explicit for her, too. She opened the freezer at the top of the refrigerator, took out a bottle of vodka, poured a tumbler full, replaced the bottle. She will carry the drink up to the bedroom, and when she hears the bath water draining in the adjoining room, she will stand at the bathroom door, which will open about six inches and she will put her hand with the glass through the opening. The glass will be removed by his hand. For my part, right now, temptation in the form of the familiar prompted me to want to take the vodka from her and carry it upstairs as in the past. The ennui of well-ordered events had a cozy appeal. I was tired; it would be a relief to fall into a familiar bed. Just then Francesca handed me the vodka, assuming, I guessed, that now I was back I would want to take my former place upstairs.

"I must leave," I said, adding, "I no longer belong here."

"Yes, of course. I'll call a cab. I hope you know what you're doing. You'll never find another man as decent as your husband."

"Empty virtue repels me."

"If you knew the world as I do, you would think twice."

"I can only think once. I will get to know the world."

"There's another thing you should know."

"And that is—?"

"Your driver's name is Joe."

For the first time in this house I laughed out loud.

JOURNEY TO PORQUIS

When at last I stood in front of the wicket I couldn't think of the name of the place.

"Truth to tell I've never been on a train," I confessed to the ticket agent, laughing lightly.

"Your destination, where do you want to go?" he demanded, frowning deeply.

The station was hot and crowded and I was holding up the line.

"The name, the name please."

I mumbled my name.

"The name of the place you want to take the train to!"

"Porquis, looks like Pourquoi, why, why would I want to go there, I don't really, you see . . . "

Downstairs I went on talking to myself. I was now at the end of a long line beside Track Number Four, facing a desk which seemed to be afloat in a sea of marble. On top of the desk was a sign, *Northern Express—Reservations*.

" . . . the boys are pretty big now but still in high school, Madeleine says that she doesn't earn enough for the four of us and that I will have to do something."

It was five minutes to departure and I began to hope that the train would leave without me and I could go home and unpack, put the baloney sandwiches back in the fridge for lunch to-morrow, get back to my word processor, it's fate, Madeleine, I wasn't meant to get the job.

No such luck. I heard a smart tattoo of high heels clipping across the marble. The line turned its head, then sighed with relief when the heels climbed up on a stool behind the desk. I decided it had not been very long since she got out of bed: she was constantly raising an arm to secure the pin holding her hair up at the back, or tuck in a wayward strand that had fallen to her shoulder. And while I was imagining a story wherein she had fallen in love with some traveller and hardly slept last night, I found myself at the head of the line staring into her mascara-ringed gray eyes. I told her I am a writer and wish to sit by myself, I intend to work on this long trip, and that also I succumb to nausea if I ride backwards. She regarded me with genuine concern. "Get sick to your tummy, eh?" and made some marks on my ticket and said, "There you go."

*

There I go, Madeleine, I'm on the train, sitting up straight in a single seat, facing an empty one. I'm sure all this will be for my own good, as you've assured me again and again. You also pointed out that you can count on the fingers of one hand the number of serious writers who can support themselves by writing. No argument there: you're absolutely right.

*

Suddenly the train began to move, picked up speed and emerged from the comfort of darkness into the glare of noon. I, the writer, always ruminating, always considering alternatives, always existing elsewhere in my mind, had a vision of reaching for the duffel bag overhead, grabbing my briefcase, taking a swift stride to the door, sliding it open and jumping off. I disappear without a trace.

In the few seconds that I used my imagination instead of my feet, I lost the chance. The train was speeding through the city and it would have been suicide to jump.

The coach was full, but the seat opposite mine remained empty. On it I spread out my notebook, the manuscript of my novel-in-progress and a book to read, Calvino's *If On a Winter's Night a Traveller*. After some hesitation I took out of the briefcase a new notebook with a bright red plastic cover. It was given to me by my wife. While on the train I was to write down (only the written word, she knows, is memorable to me)—I was to write down my brilliant (her word) insights into Post-modern Fiction, so that when I am being interviewed for the job I will have cogent theories instead of my usual cynical remarks about the teaching of literature, Madeleine said.

I closed the red plastic cover over the blank page.

A young woman bent over me and whispered, "Can I get you something? from the bar? coffee? sandwich?" "No thank you very much." I looked up and discovered that she was the same young woman with the artless smile and the incorrigible dark hair. "I'll be back," she promised.

The train was moving swiftly and smoothly through the east end of the city, a district I had never seen. I am not given to walks or excursions, they interfere with writing. We came to outskirts with only a few old factories with blackened windows, the sight of which led me to think it might be salutary to have a job where the sun shines through clean glass and where I could take a deep breath of fresh air and where I would not be afraid to ride a bicycle.

All this while I have been aware of the hostess wiggling her way back and forth in the aisle with trays of tinned pop, coffee, beer. Her source of supply was in another coach, but coming or going she stopped, smiled down at me—"Would you like something?"—she smiled as she balanced her tray, a hazardous feat on high heels when the train lurched or went around a curve. What struck me, the observant writer, was the nature of her smile: it was fixed.

*

So, Madeleine, I'm on my way. Any writer will tell you that the genesis of a story lies in staring and has nothing to do with personal interest in beautiful young women, the staring is for character study only. You said some funny things about the blond owner of the gift shop across the street. "She looks like her place mats, all white and pink." You said, "Seriously though, you'll have to do something else besides stare out the window." *Seriously though* was the unkindest cut: as if rejection slips, headaches and nausea aren't serious.

*

As the landscape changed I tried to visualize myself out there somewhere with a job: as a bus driver, driving; as a farmer, farming; as a teacher, teaching. Front and centre in each picture—on the wheel of the bus, on the tractor in the field, on the desk in the classroom—were walls of books, papers everywhere and my word processor.

My neck hurt from holding my head, unmoving, against the window. I turned my head. The silent couple directly across the aisle were looking out their window. I had a mnemonic flash of them when they came into the coach at Barrie, she striding ahead, looking angry, and he walking behind her with his head down.

"Don't ever do that again!" I heard her say.

I reached for my notebook.

"What, what did I do?"

"You know very well. Don't do it again."

"I don't know, tell me, what did I do wrong?"

"You know very well ... last night ... "

"What, what, last night ... "

*

If I were to tell you, Madeleine, what you did last night, you would regard me with the same sad bewilderment as that man facing me.

Last night, Madeleine, there was a total yielding of your mind and body to brushing your hair. You raise your bare arm, holding the brush so tightly your knuckles show white. Your skin in the mirror is luminous. You bring the hairbrush down, stroke your long hair to the very ends, bring your arm up again, lower it; long slow motions, again and again, up, down, up, down, with an inexpressible grace in the unbroken motion. Then you yawned and examined your fingernails.

*

In the confines of this steel coach, restricted to this one seat, there was a loss of choice, as in a prison. Yet, paradoxically, I was moving swiftly in space. A different sense, no longer rooted in place, took hold of me.

The train slowed down, the next station was announced, the train stopped, movement all around, murmur of voices, the train started, picked up speed, the miles unrolled, my thoughts accelerated. I began to write:

> At this time of year the sunlight is stark. The countryside is revealed in sharp angles, shadows are long, the earth lies fallow. Buildings appear for an instant only—tidy brick farm houses, old barns, wooden houses newly pain-ted, abandoned rust-red railway stations. Children halt their play to wave at us. The train whistle announces our northern passage through woods and past lakes; the terrain shows outcroppings of rock. It is only September and already the forest floor is covered with golden leaves, the birch trees gleam white. Here and there in the hills, intimations of the winter to come: maples with top leaves frost-bitten into a bright red or a deep purple.

On this train I wouldn't have to wrack my heart and soul for that elusive fiction: stories awaited me. There they sat, my captive characters—women in pairs chatted away; people played cards and drank beer; young people listened to earphones, lovers sat very still, her head on his shoulder; a potato-chip salesman was at this very moment going up and down the aisle handing out samples. Then there were the couples—my familiars I began to call them—in life's three stages: the young marrieds with eyes only for each other; the middle-aged ones across the aisle, no longer angry; and an old white-haired pair, who rarely exchanged a word; and, of course, the ever-smiling Lucy.

Words, phrases and exclamations reached me. I couldn't write fast enough. I put Calvino and my work-in-progress back in the briefcase and put my feet up.

There was a new feeling, a quickening of my heart beat, when, in a flash, it came to me that I was on the verge of finding the bridge between literature and life. Dostoievsky said, "Every day I have to decide whether to live or to write." Here the decision is made for me: I have nowhere to go, yet the train carries me along with others on mysterious journeys.

Lingering at my side, smiling down at me, was the hostess, trayless.

"Do you mind?" He sat down, the young man who had been standing behind her. "Do you mind if Raffaelo sits here?"—I lowered my feet—"he hasn't got a reservation." She put his plastic bag, marked *President's Choice* beside my duffel bag overhead. I sized him up as a man very attractive to women, with his lean frame, long legs and head of dark curls.

The train had been in and out of South River. I ate my baloney sandwich and wondered how long I would have to face this silent enigma who kept staring at a spot over my head. Suddenly, without moving an eyelid, without as much as a clearing of his throat, he announced into the distant air:

"A man who lives a whole year in a place and doesn't ask a girl out. I stayed in a house where there were three girls and I didn't ask any of them out. I worked in a post office, lots of girls, didn't so much as ask one of them out for coffee. I worked in a muffler shop, lots of girls come in with busted mufflers and I didn't ask any of them for a date. A whole year. Not once. Didn't ask a girl out."

"You're a young guy, good looking, they wouldn't turn you down."

"A whole year. A coward."

"What are you afraid of?"

"Her."

"Who?"

"A girl. I asked my doctor if he had courage pills. He gave me something to relieve anxiety, he said. The pills made me sleepy. What girl would go out with a sleepy guy?"

Still looking over my head he asked,

"Have you got a girl?"

"Yes, she's my wife."

"I would like a wife."

His blind stare shifted to my notebook.

"Are you writing it down?"

"On no," I lied.

"That's good, I wouldn't want anyone to find out that I lived in a place a whole year and never asked a girl out."

"What about the hostess? Why don't you ask her out?"

"Lucy? I mean a real date, not someone who's like a sister."

When the loudspeaker announced *Next Stop North Bay* Raffaelo stood up. "Time for exercise, you gotta keep fit if you're going to ask a girl for a date." I watched him run beside the track. He was back before the train started up. He stood on the seat, reached for my duffel bag. "This yours?" and threw it down into my lap, climbed up and stretched out his long frame on the baggage rack.

Then the hostess, she'd become Lucy to me, was sitting across from me. She kicked off her shoes.

"That Raf! Does he bother you? He thinks he lives on the *Northern*, that we are his family. We go along with him; he has to have someone; he has to have a place he can call home." We looked up at him; his eyes were fixed on the ceiling.

"He used to live in a halfway house," Lucy said, "can you imagine having to live in a house that's half-way? Halfway to what? At least on a train you're always going somewhere."

I was writing rapidly. About Raffaelo. I was inventing a life for him. I had him born into a large family in Haileybury, which we have just passed. He will grow up, like myself, on a farm, the only child of Methodist parents. I ascribe to him my own years of loneliness, hours of reading, years of acne and agonies over girls. He will go to college in a small town, then to the Big City. Pleasures delayed will be realized. Perhaps he'll be a college professor or an international spy, or both.

The words flowed.

We had just pulled out of Temagami; the lights in the coach came on; outside there was a bit of last light through the tops of trees; all about me there were fitful noises as we settled in for the evening. *Haileybury, Timmins, Smooth Rock* were announced, people got off, but nobody came aboard.

By night-time the coach was empty except for me, my three couples who were dozing, Raffaelo snoring lightly overhead, Lucy asleep on two empty seats, the dividing arm raised out of the way, a small pile of magazines under her head and a coat over her shoulders.

I closed my eyes and wished the train would never stop. I dreaded the end of my journey. We were due in Porquis at two in the morning. I would spend the rest of the night between cold sheets in a motel, and at nine the next morning I would face the Search Committee of Kapawanooka University. The Committee will consist of three or five or more, it's always an odd number, I know: I've been through a number of these interviews. It will go something like this:

"Your curriculum vitae lists twelve addresses in the past ten years. Do you have difficulties in adjustment to your habitat?"

"Not at all. The habitat won't adjust to me, I work at night, I pace the floor."

I can imagine that while they are clearing throats and fiddling with papers, my streak of perversity will fill the silence:

"We live in three rooms over a fish and chip store." I lean across the table, hold out my arm under their noses, "Can you smell the oil? I don't smell it any more because I smell oil all the time. Mind you, the oil is never rancid, it is changed frequently. They make the best fish and chips in the city. People come from all over. On Friday nights a line extends down the street and around the block. A policeman keeps it orderly."

The chairman looks sympathetic. He speaks with a Scottish brogue.

"Why have you remained in this aura of oil?"

"The rent is cheap."

"Still, the adjustments must be considerable. How do you maintain creativity under these conditions?"

"It's a good place to write. The building is quiet in the mornings and at night."

I don't remember falling asleep, but just as one sometimes wakes just before the alarm goes off, so I sat up and looked at my watch five minutes before the scheduled stop at Porquis.

The train did not stop, although *Porquis Next Stop* came clearly over the loudspeaker. It kept chugging along, its rhythm unbroken. More stations were announced—names I had paid no attention to, not even while I dozed, my duffel bag ready, everything back in my briefcase, prepared to get off the moment the train stopped. Now I heard *Smooth Rock Falls, Englehart, Cobalt*—the order of towns reversed.

I woke Lucy.

"What's happening? I have to get to Porquis, we're going backwards!"

"Not to worry. You want to write, don't you? Trust me."

She patted my hand. I was trembling. I stared at her, at her smile: it was a mysterious smile that one associates with idiots and saints.

Hours later the train did stop. At *North Bay*. Raffaelo climbed down, stepped on my duffel bag, nodded to me; we got out in pitch dark and ran around the station which was lit with a feeble light in a doorway. I could see that the train now consisted only of the engine and our coach.

Powassan, Trout Creek, Burks Falls. The announcements continued in their reverse order. In *Toronto* I was prepared to get off, but the train did not stop there. I heard next *Barrie, Orillia, Gravenhurst,* and knew we were headed north again.

I was frightened, but strangely happy. There was no reason for me to be concerned. The train chugged north, the train chugged south, back and forth. I kept writing. Every once in a while one of my characters would sit opposite and ask how the work was going. "Just fine, just fine," I would answer. And it was. Once I ran out of paper, out of ink in the ball point. Lucy brought me a blue binder filled with lined paper and two pens, one with red ink. We stopped only at North Bay, where the townspeople awaited us with hot food, extra blankets and sweaters for Raffaelo and me for our jogging.

Lucy brought drinks and sandwiches when we wanted them. Her smile, however, was no longer broad and fixed: it was slight and sweet, like that of a sleeping child having a happy dream. Often she sat at the back, bent over a thick book and writing on lined paper in a blue binder like mine. Once when I stopped to watch her, she looked up and said simply, "Tibetan."

The days and nights passed, winter came, sun shone on clean white snow, we kept going north, then south, back and forth. Up north the black flies were bad in June; there were times in summer when we could barely jog along the tracks at North Bay; then it was Fall again with the woods in glorious colour.

Before the onset of cold weather, my three couples came over, one pair at a time, and asked how much longer I needed them. I arranged to have the young marrieds get off at Cobalt to stay with her parents until the baby came in December; and I found a nursing home for the elderly couple where they could stay together in Huntsville.

The middle-aged couple across the aisle were closest in age to Madeleine and me. I asked them how they'd feel if he, the husband, were to join a scientific expedition to the Falkland Islands for two years. He beamed and said he'd always wanted to go to Argentina and that was pretty close. The second week of November he got off at Toronto. "Wait for me," he begged his wife, "I love only you." She began to cry. I offered her freedom from housework, any career she wanted. "It's too late," she said, "you should have thought of that when I was young. I need him now, to grow old along with me, the best is yet to be." She refused to be consoled, wouldn't eat the food Lucy brought her. In January, cold as it was, she got off at Moose Factory. "He can go on measuring the wind for the rest of his life for all I care. I don't want him back." She pointed to my notebook. "Do what you like with him."

I heard the usual *Toronto Next Stop* but it no longer meant anything to me. I kept writing as I waited for the now-familiar pull forward when the train started. When there was no motion I looked around. There was Raffaelo in the aisle, wearing his windbreaker and holding on to his *President's Choice* shopping bag.

"You don't have to worry about me any more," he said, "There's lots of girls in Toronto."

Lucy came up behind him with a small suitcase and a pleased smile.

"You got lots written, eh? Take care, see you ... "

*

Some days I get to thinking about Lucy and Raffaelo, and in that aimless rumination I see them still on the train. Logically I tell myself that they now live in my novel and it won't be necessary for me to go back on the *Northern Express* to be with them. And between reading and listening to Madeleine, who keeps threatening to leave me, and wondering, not too enthusiastically, whether I should teach night school or give English lessons, or do nothing but write, I simply take a long walk to the east end of the city and go into a dark bar where no one shows surprise at anything.

THE MAN WITHOUT MEMORIES

Alfred Mulgrave is at the windows, his left hand is placed firmly on the horse cast in bronze, the other hand raises the binoculars resting on his chest and focuses them on his parking lot twenty-two storeys below; it is his parking lot not only because that is where his Buick is parked, but also because he owns the very pavement on which all those cars are sitting; he surveys the large square lot with pride, everything in order, the cement smooth and clean, not a scrap of paper, the white lines freshly painted, marking spaces for 160 cars if each is properly parked. Mulgrave raises his binoculars slightly and tips them toward the farther distance, to the fieldstone house, the word nestling comes to him, the little house nestling in the northwest end of the lot, it must be 8:30 now, there is Helga, husband off to work, children off to school, there she is, an apron covering the front of a print dress, sweeping the three front steps, shaking out the mat, oblivious, as she is supposed to be, to the cars driving around her.

The motherly woman in an apron taking care of his home.

*

What do you think I like it no neighbours, Henry standing in the middle of the empty parking lot, all this space, he has to shout because Helga has wasted no time and is heading for the stone house at the end of the lot, it's Sunday, she shouts back, that's why the lot's empty, the chain is still on, and Henry, you'd think he'd get one of those electronic arms that go up and down; by now Helga has unlocked the door and has disappeared even as Henry is telling her that they'll have to leave the van out on the street overnight; Henry now inside the house finds Helga upstairs in the bedroom, he, excited, the whole house is ours for one whole year, the whole place is ours; Helga has pulled down the green cloth window blinds between the ruffled curtains, there are three windows facing the office building; she, that Mulgrave isn't going to see us in bed, where Henry is already stretched out on top of the patched quilt, bouncing, saying, the springs have no spring, and Helga beside him but between the sheets says, the mattress is lumpy.

The sun this Sunday at one point is on the stone house and Henry and Helga are in a kitchen suddenly bright, they make no remarks about the wooden ice-box with its massive block of ice inside a separate compartment, although Henry said to himself then and said later, each and every time, the ice-man cometh; they are silent before a tall white cupboard with a porcelain counter edged in blue diamond shapes, they open two little doors at the bottom and find tin canisters marked *flour, tea* and *sugar*; they see a long shallow white enamel sink with exposed metal pipes beneath. Henry, this is what my father must have walked out on, I've come full circle you think you're making momentous decisions to become a full-time writer, you're going to change your life dramatically, and all you're doing is going back to where you started from, and she, examining pots and pans in a squat cupboard beside the sink, I'm going to be doing what my mother hated doing, and Henry, my mother never complained, even when my father walked out, and she, I've never really kept house before. Henry was looking out the kitchen window at the parking lot, at the gray and spotted pavement, patches of oil glistened where the sun hit, otherwise the lot was in shadows cast by the surrounding buildings. He, it's the best part of the city, now that we're in a real house maybe I can get the kids back, wait'll they see this, their own rooms, and Helga points out she hopes his wife will agree, that her daughter can take the bus from St. Catharines, without kids it's no deal, but Henry, not listening, remarks that Dickens called a home an island in a nasty world, and she, an island in a nasty parking lot, adding quickly, because Henry turned around, looking uncertain, let's check out the parlor, that's what they called the living room, didn't they, the parlor, I'm sure it's authentic Depression, like the rest of this place, it's going to be easy to live out his imagined past and write his happy family script, and Henry repeated that his mother never complained, adding, we'll never pull it off if you're going to be cynical, but she is walking about pointing to this and that, the anti-macassars on the overstuffed furniture, the china figurines, the sepia faces in dark varnished oval frames, you'll have to help me with the dusting, she said, and Henry, I'm supposed to be the *pater familias*, I don't do dusting, then quickly, just joking, we'll work something out, Mulgrave can't see everywhere with those binoculars; listen, I don't know any more about family life than you do, there'll be lots of research, you like to read, it's a nice walk from here to the Metro Library, something to do while the kids are in school; and she, no, that won't work, I have to be at home, in case of emergency the children must know their mother is there, that's what he said.

*

Alfred Mulgrave is at the windows, his left hand holding on to the bronze horse, in his other hand are the binoculars, a long loving look at the stone house, the lenses are inched along the stones, one by one, the stones speak to him of tradition, an upward tilt to admire the three gabled windows on the second floor, downwards to the small green lawns on either side of the steps, extending all the way back to the rear of the house, protected by a white iron fence, a small replica of the iron fence surrounding Osgoode Hall, and an iron gate through which you move in one direction, then turn through another opening towards the house, the kind of gate designed to keep out cows. Memo: have roses clambering up a trellis on either side of the steps. Only a man of vision could have located the little stone house, had it dug up, transported a hundred kilometers; to have dug a foundation for this house right on his own parking lot; to have had the first floor gutted and the kitchen, the dining room and the parlor made to face his office windows; the wiring, the plumbing; find authentic Depression furnishings, plant a lawn, locate a foundry for the iron fence and gate—it took some doing, but he did create a home he could be proud of.

*

So the next day, Henry and Helga in Mulgrave's office, the children weren't with them, they're with my mother Helga said until we get settled, and Mulgrave, but there's nothing to settle, everything is in, furniture, linens, everything, but our personal things, they're in too, even clothing, in your sizes for the farm, 1928 to 1932, my early years, for the city 1932 to 1942, my adolescence, and then began the embarrassment of having to read from a list headed Personal Items, Male, and Personal Items, Female; after all, he reminded them you will have to live as people did fifty years ago, there must be nothing fictitious in my autobiography, there will be no tv, although I did find a 1932 Philco radio, vintage books only; for my part, Mulgrave assured them, certain memories were not important enough to burden the mind or I would have recalled them; however, for purposes of my autobiography I shall observe your family life and make notes which Henry will elaborate into professional prose; above all, avoid melodrama, there is nothing missing in my life, waving an arm around, on every one of the 42 floors of this building, behind every door, in every cubicle, there is evidence of my many achievements, which I find more satisfying than dreams of happiness.

*

Well, here we are, what do you think? I like it, plunk in the middle of this great city, great theatres, great restaurants, great shops, everything, no neighbours, alone at night, it'll be like camping in the wilderness, you and I and space, imagine, all this is ours, libraries, too, you can walk down in ten minutes to the Reference Library, we'll have a wonderful year, we will be an "island in a nasty world"; and Helga looking from Henry to the parking lot outside the window, back and forth, sees Henry and his eagerness and sees also the slow parade of cars on the lot, admits that the idea of an island in a nasty world is poetic and appealing right now, then Henry says it is only a figure of speech by Charles Dickens; and she turns from the window and says, just when I think you are really telling me something I need to hear, it turns out to be a quote, I never know whether it's you or some other writer; and Henry, I've started research, that's all, I have to get the right tone for his memoirs, I think I've got it, he wants a dream of "living in a cozy little knot of human beings who love us more than they love anybody else," and she, nothing wrong with a dream like that, and he, sorry, that's a quote too.

*

At this time of day all the curtains are drawn against his view. Mulgrave has agreed to specific hours for watching family life, a concession to Henry-Helga, who stood before him a week after their arrival, they were no longer the amiable couple of the interview, Henry glaring, you haven't got enough money for this kind of invasion of privacy, and Helga, red-cheeked and bright-eyed, we have lives, too, you know, lives of our own to live, not only the

lives you want from us; and Mulgrave, please don't cry, I
see no reason for secrecy in a kitchen where you cook or
in a dining room where you eat or quiet family times in
the parlor, and Henry, we have our rights; and Mulgrave
concluded that this kind of petty self-assertion, all these
platitudes about violations of privacy, merely attested to his
shrewd choice: they were a typical middle class couple of
no worldly experience. A new contract would be drawn up,
naming exact hours Mulgrave could see their family life.
They relaxed, Henry said he found Mulgrave's notes help-
ful and Helga invited him to dinner some night, not for
turnips and shepherd's pie, but for wine and gourmet del-
icacies. They left pleased with themselves.

A passion for safety.

*

Again the pull towards the windows, Mulgrave pre-
pares to enter a memory, if not his own, any memory will
do, but today he elaborates on the morning ritual; no calls
he says into the inter-com, then, as if expecting a visitor,
he washes up, combs his hair, buttons his jacket, wipes the
lens of the binoculars, and holding on to the sculpture at
his left, trains the binoculars on the solid stone house at
the northwest end of the parking lot, facing the windows
of the kitchen, dining room, parlor and the master bedroom
upstairs, it is 8:45, the white kitchen curtains are parted, he
can see Helga standing at the gas stove, stirring something,
it is a hot nourishing breakfast; then the children come in
one by one, washed and dressed fresh, the boys' hair
brushed down, the girl's long hair tied with a red ribbon
at the back, which is visible each time the child turns her
head, then Henry, yawning, dressed for the office in a dark
suit and white shirt and muted tie, joins the children at the
table, he speaks to them and they reply, and when Helga
sits down for her breakfast, the children become quiet while

their parents have a conversation about the day ahead, which gives the observer an opportunity to make a few quick notes; then, breakfast over, the children gather their books held together with leather straps, Helga hands them little lunch pails (an anachronism here, Mulgrave wonders), kisses them one by one, they leave, walking carefully, single file, across the parking lot, against the arrows to the left of the aisle, as instructed, exiting at the walkway on Heath Street, then five minutes later Henry kisses Helga and leaves, carrying his briefcase, exiting at the walkway on Yonge Street, where, in the notebook, he takes a street car south to Wellington Street and walks over to Bay Street to his office,where he has a position writing geological reports for a company promoting stocks in a gold mine. (Henry came up with this idea for a scenario when the farm is lost during the Depression but the father, they discussed, could always find work because of his fine appearance and superior intelligence.)

Helga can be seen clearing the dishes, washing them in a dishpan in the sink, after which she emerges from the front door, an apron over her housedress, in cold weather and on the farm she will wear a heavy cardigan, and all in full view she proceeds to sweep the front steps and shake the mat, indifferent to the cars that pass on all sides as she wields the broom and when she is finished she stands for a moment and looks into the distance, making Mulgrave reach for his notebook and rapidly write "gazing out at the fields yielding their growth to the morning sun," Mulgrave has no problems with chronology, after all, memory operates outside time, he has several hard-covered notebooks, one of which will be for the farm at Elora before the Depression drove the family to the City; in the meantime Helga has re-entered the house.

The kitchen curtains closed.

*

For one thing, the dark blinds at the bedroom windows hung slightly away from the glass, bits of light from the parking lot floodlight penetrated the room, Henry in bed beside Helga in the semi-darkness knows she is awake, wants to comfort her, tells her, we can love each other anywhere, we've slept together in stranger places, remember the time you were locked out and we slept in the shoe store where I worked? so that Helga drew a little closer, she, I can't even read in bed with that silly little lamp, and Henry, that's the way it used to be, saving on electricity, I suppose, it's an authentic lamp of the period, Henry wanting to hold her, nothing has changed between us, then after a while he asked what's the matter and Helga said I just can't relax, I keep hearing motors and car doors slamming, we're supposed to be living in a farm house 'way out in the country, in peace and silence, he, we could get ear plugs, and she, then we might as well stay in separate rooms if I can't hear you sleep, he, you mean I snore? she, no, no, you make sounds I'm used to, I can tell by your breathing if you're having a good dream or a bad one, or how your writing's going, your breathing keeps changing and I want to hear it, even in my sleep, and he, drawing away, says, it's just for a year.

*

After weeks of moving curtains back and forth for Mulgrave's binoculars, Helga one day drew them shut with studied carelessness, so that a space was left between the inside edges through which she could look out on the car park; it was cold, the ground was covered with fresh snow that had fallen during the night, it was enough to make people linger in their warm cars, there is that gray Oldsmobile Cutlass again, driven by an elderly man with a daughter at his side, but just now he leans over and puts his mouth on hers in a long kiss; Helga watches them leave the lot through the Yonge Street walkway, notes how the young woman moves with controlled deliberation as she keeps pace with his slow, stately walk; and later, when it's time to open all the curtains and drapes and start that business of the kids' homework and preparing dinner, Helga is still at the window and sees the old man and the young girl return with boxes and bags and this time the young woman leans over to kiss his cheek.

Never-ending stories of men and women and cars, if only people were not so predictable, life imitating daytime "Soaps," all the same she was pulled to take another look, and yet another, through the spaces, and when it became imperative to know what was going on in the cars in the more distant parts of the lot, she bought binoculars. In her sights now is a couple in a white Audi 5000, his hands gripping the top of the steering wheel show French cuffs at the wrists, beside him is a woman, her coat open, a purse on her lap, she is crying and digging into her purse for fresh tissues, he is staring straight ahead, then he lights a cigarette, then another, which he offers to her, she shakes her head and keeps blowing her nose, he keeps smoking and staring, she keeps crying.

A silence not seen on tv.

*

The kitchen curtains closed.

He went on making notes, snippets really, his mother coming down the stairs, from one year to the next, she comes down the stairs, and when she gives him a hug and a kiss, her skin is slightly moist, but no more than a flower in bloom is moist; you cannot put down in words such desires for all the world to read, and her skin has a fragrance of its own, he can feel and smell her skin, his pen stays in mid-air; but he cannot see her features, and trying to put a face on the body was like being under an anaesthetic counting backwards from ten, he halts at number seven, he has a vision, a woman weeping, don't stop now, the doctor urges, go on, six, five, four . . .

A desire for oblivion.

Acknowledgements

The stories in this collection have previously been published in the following magazines and anthologies:

"Circle of Fifths": *Saturday Night*, 1976.

"The Means": *Tamarack Review*, 1977.

"My Mother's Luck": *Jewish Dialogue*, 1968; *Fireweed*, 1982; *The Best of Fireweed* (Fireweed, 1986).

"Quadrille": *Jewish Dialogue*, 1975.

"Causation": *Small Wonders* (C.B.C. Enterprises, 1982); *The Anthology Anthology* (C.B.C. Enterprises, 1984); *The Oxford Book of Canadian Short Stories in English* (Oxford, 1986); *More Stories by Canadian Women* (Oxford, 1987); *Mots et Mirages* (C.B.C. Enterprises/Editions Fides, 1987).

"Surprise": *Canadian Forum*, 1968.

"L'Envoi": *Canadian Forum*, 1981.

"A View from the Roof": *Jewish Dialogue*, 1972.

"Hold That Tiger": *Toronto Life*, 1980; *The Spice Box* (Lester & Orpen Dennys, 1985).

"What Happened to Ravel's Bolero?": *The Fiddlehead*, 1983; *Canadian Short Stories, series 4* (Oxford, 1985).

"Homecoming": *Tamarack Review*, 1979.

"Journey to Porquis": *The Fiddlehead*, 1989.

"The Man Without Memories": *Canadian Women Studies*, 1987, *Books in Canada*, 1987.